DAUGHTERS OF THE MOON

the
secret
scroll

Also in the
DAUGHTERS OF THE MOON
series:

DAUGHTERS OF THE MOON

the secret scroll

LYNNE EWING

HYPERION/NEW YORK

First Edition
9 10 8
Printed in the United States of America

Library of Congress Cataloging-in-Publication Data
Ewing, Lynne.
The secret scroll Lynne Ewing.—1st ed.
p.   cm. — (Daughters of the moon ; #4)
Summary: Catty, a girl with the power to travel back in time, inherits a secret scroll that
will help her defeat the evil Atrox.
ISBN-13: 978-0-7868-0709-3
ISBN-10: 0-7868-0709-1
[1. Supernatural—Fiction. 2. Time travel—Fiction. 3. Los Angeles (Calif.)—Fiction.]
I. Title.
PZ7.E965 Se 2001
[Fic]—dc21   00-53924

Visit www.hyperionteens.com

For Mair Jack Mayesh

Long ago, darkness reigned over the night. People were afraid and remained inside their shelters from sundown until sunrise. The goddess Selene saw their fear and gave light to their nocturnal world by driving her moon chariot across the starry sky. She followed her brother Helios, who rode the sun and caught his shining rays on her magnificent silver chariot, then cast them down to earth as moonbeams. She felt pride in the way the earthlings were comforted by her light.

But one night when she had abandoned her chariot to walk upon the earth, she noticed that in times of trouble many people lost all hope. Their despair bewildered her. After considering their plight, she knew how she could make her moon the greatest gift from the gods.

From then on she drove around the earth and each night caught her brother's rays from a different angle. This way the face of the moon was everchanging. People watched the moon decrease in light every night, until it could no longer be seen from the earth. Then after three nights of darkness, a crescent sliver returned and the moon increased in light until it was fully illuminated as before. Selene did this to remind people that their darkest times can lead them to their brightest.

The ancients understood Selene's gift in the lunar phases. Each night when they gazed at the moon, they knew Selene was telling them to never give up hope.

CHAPTER ONE

ATTY STOPPED ON the cement step and stared at the lettering on the side of the building. She wanted to turn and run, but Kendra took her hand to reassure her. The traffic from the nearby freeway filled the hot afternoon with a constant drone like surf rushing to shore. She wished she were at the beach. Anyplace but here.

It had been the most terrible day ever even before the phone call. She had laughingly told Kendra that the only good thing about it was that it couldn't get any worse. Then the phone rang.

Now all her problems at school suddenly seemed unimportant.

"We better go in," Kendra coaxed. She pressed her lips tightly together, resolute, and adjusted her purse over her shoulder. The phone call had upset her, too, but her way to handle anything bad was to take action.

Catty nodded and started toward the Los Angeles County Coroner's office.

Kendra gently touched her arm. "It's probably not your mother anyway."

Catty looked down at the brown envelope on which she had scrawled the woman's name. Zoe Reese. Was that her mother? She whispered the name again, hoping it would jog a memory. It didn't.

"I'm sure it's a mistake." Kendra frowned behind her dark glasses. She was a large woman with high cheekbones and long brown hair streaked with gray.

Catty loved her. Kendra was the only mother she had ever known. She had often wondered what her life had been before Kendra had found her walking along the highway in the Arizona desert when she was six years old. She hadn't even known her name when Kendra had stopped the car that day and asked if she was okay. "Catty" was the name Kendra had given her. She only had two memories of the time before that moment: one of a crash, the other of an explosion. None of her real mother. Would she finally have some answers now? She wondered if she would be able to see herself in her mother's face.

Maybe now she'd be able to piece together her past and find out where she came from. Then, unexpectedly, a feeling of hurt surged through her, reopening a childhood wound. If her mother had lived in Los Angeles all these years, why had she never contacted her?

Catty followed Kendra across a long cement slab that led to the double glass doors. When they stepped inside the coroner's office, a rush of cold air and the alcohol smell of antiseptics closed tightly around them. Catty's hands began to tremble, and she pushed them deep inside her jeans pockets.

Kendra's shoes squeaked on the highly polished floor as she stepped past the case of citations and plaques to the reception window. She slid her sunglasses on top of her head and pulled on her red-framed reading glasses, then tapped her finger impatiently on the glass partition. Her gold rings flashed and bracelets jangled on her thick wrist.

"Your office called my daughter," Kendra started.

The receptionist looked up with a practiced expression somewhere between a smile and pity, then she saw Catty and her face changed. "They called her?"

Kendra nodded. "To inform my daughter that her mother had died."

The receptionist's pale face went blank.

Kendra cleared her throat. "I'm not her biological mother," she explained.

"Oh," the receptionist answered, and that same sad and pleasant expression returned to her face. "You'll need to contact a funeral home and make arrangements with them to claim the body."

Kendra pressed her hand against the glass. Her nails were long and painted red. "But I don't understand what makes you think that woman is her mother. I spoke with the person on the phone and all they gave me was a name and an address—"

"They never call without proof," the receptionist asserted calmly.

"Maybe if you'd let us see her," Kendra suggested. "Perhaps we'd be able to see a resemblance."

Catty started. She didn't think she had the courage to look at the woman's face. Tears pressed into her eyes. She tried to swallow, but her mouth was too dry and her tongue made an odd click in the back of her throat. She had always thought about seeing her mother someday, but this was not the way she had imagined it.

"I'm sorry." The receptionist seemed truly concerned. "We're not designed to accommodate viewing. You'll have to make arrangements with a funeral home. They'll let you view—"

"You're not understanding." Kendra tried to

keep a smile on her face to hide her frustration. She clasped the beads hanging around her neck, and Catty knew she was mentally reciting her mantra, searching for calm. When she spoke again, her voice seemed more serene. "I have no proof that this woman is my daughter's biological mother, so why should we make arrangements for her?"

"They had to have had proof." The receptionist's voice had taken on a defensive tone. "They wouldn't randomly call someone."

"I understand. All I am asking is that you show me that same proof." Kendra's arm reached out and pulled Catty tight against her. The scents of sandalwood and heather clung sweetly to Kendra's dress. "Why don't you have a seat while I get some answers?" Kendra whispered to her.

Catty nodded and headed for one of the purple chairs lined against the wall. She sat down and tried to concentrate on the day, hoping her problems at school might distract her from the argument Kendra was having with the receptionist.

Her stomach pinched just thinking about her new boyfriend, Chris. She had thought everything was perfect between them, and then today at school he had seemed so distant. She wondered if he had been trying to find the words to break up with her. What had happened to the attentive guy who was so open with her? At lunch he had shrugged and said he couldn't stay with her. And they always ate in the cafeteria together. After school he had acted indifferent about meeting her at Planet Bang. He told her he would call. But he hadn't so far.

That alone was enough to make the day a disaster. But even earlier, it had started badly. During first period, Mr. Hall had passed back the last geometry tests. She had received a D.

Then right after class her best friend Vanessa had gotten mad at her because Catty had said some nice things about Michael Saratoga and his band in front of Vanessa's creepy new boyfriend, Toby. Everyone knew Vanessa still liked Michael, so why was she wasting time with Toby, anyway? There was no way Vanessa could convince Catty that she really liked him. When Vanessa flirted with him her eyes seemed to be looking for someone else, someone like Michael. And when Toby tried to hold her close, she never looked totally comfortable with it. Vanessa had only become more angry when Catty pointed this out to her. Too bad Toby had been standing nearby and listening.

Catty sighed. Before the phone call from the coroner's office, she had planned to smooth things over with Vanessa tonight at Planet Bang. They had been best friends for a long time, and no way was she going to let a guy come between them.

But then Kendra had surprised her. She wouldn't relent and take her off restriction. Since Kendra had started teaching the night Latin class at UCLA, she had relied on Catty to watch her bookstore in the evenings and punctuality had suddenly become very important to her. Twice Catty had made Kendra late, and the third time Kendra did the unthinkable and actually put her on restriction. Restriction was something new for

Catty. Kendra had always let her do whatever she wanted because she knew Catty wasn't like other kids.

She glanced at Kendra now and felt a surge of gratitude. Kendra continually tried to help Catty understand her strange ability. She had even encouraged Catty to use what Kendra called her gift. What would have happened to her if someone else had stopped that day at the desert? She hated to imagine what her life could have been. She might have ended up in some sideshow or as an exhibit in the Smithsonian.

From the beginning, Kendra had assumed that Catty was from some distant planet and that her extraordinary power was actually a form of teleportation used by her people. She had cautioned Catty not to tell anyone about her unusual skill. And Catty hadn't until she met Vanessa. She had known immediately that Vanessa was different, too, when she saw the silver moon amulet hanging around her neck. It was identical to the one Catty wore. Catty looked down at her amulet now and studied the face of the moon etched in the metal. She had been wearing the charm when Kendra found her. Now, sparkling in the fluorescent lights, it didn't look silver, but opalescent. She never took it off.

Kendra turned and glanced at her, her eyes asking if she was okay. Catty tried to smile back, but her lips curled in a sad imitation of one.

She wished she could find the courage to tell Kendra the truth. She hated keeping any secret from her. But the words never came. It was probably easier to believe in people from outer space than to accept what Catty really was, anyway. She sometimes thought Kendra would feel disappointed if she learned the truth. Kendra was always on the Internet trying to find out more about UFO sightings, Area 51, and Roswell. She seemed to enjoy the research.

Catty studied Kendra now. Her cheeks had taken on an angry red blush and her fingers frantically worked at the beads hanging around her neck. Would Kendra even believe her if she did tell her the truth . . . that she was a goddess, a

Daughter of the Moon, on Earth to protect people from the Followers of an ancient evil called the Atrox?

Who she was had remained a mystery to her until just a few months ago, when she had been kidnapped by Followers, before she even knew what they were. Fortunately, Vanessa and two other Daughters, Jimena and Serena, had rescued her. Vanessa had told her the truth then, but Catty hadn't believed it until she had met Maggie Craven, a retired schoolteacher.

"Tu es dea, filia lunae," Maggie had told her in Latin. Catty had been surprised she understood the words, but she had. "You are a Goddess, a Daughter of the Moon." The words still sent a thrill of excitement through her.

Kendra's voice pulled her back from her thoughts.

"What is your proof?" Kendra raised her voice in exasperation, and the words echoed around the small room.

Catty stood and walked back to Kendra, hoping her presence might calm her.

The receptionist picked up a pencil and began twirling it nervously between her fingers. "The person who called you should have answered all of your questions."

"We won't leave until you show us proof." Kendra's voice was firm.

Catty rested her hand on Kendra's arm. The muscles felt tense.

"I'll call Security," the receptionist threatened.

Wrong thing to say, Catty thought and shot a warning look at Kendra.

"Call Security." Kendra smiled broadly. She knew how to make a scene. She relished the opportunity.

The receptionist must have had a lot of experience with the public. She seemed to sense that Kendra's challenge was not a bluff. Instead of reaching for the phone, she set her pencil down with a sudden snap and stood. She marched from her enclosure to a door marked *property release*, knocked briefly, then stepped inside.

Kendra gave Catty a questioning look. "Should we follow?" But her shoes were already squeaking across the floor after the receptionist. She caught the door before it closed and propped it open.

Catty followed into the overly cooled room.

The receptionist spoke in whispers to a shorter woman. The smaller woman gathered a brown envelope from a filing cabinet and handed it to the receptionist, who pulled something from deep inside.

"Here." The receptionist showed Kendra and Catty a worn piece of notebook paper. "This was found in the woman's pocket."

Kendra held it in her large hands.

"It's a geometry test," Catty muttered. "My geometry test."

Kendra readjusted her reading glasses and examined the paper closely. Catty looked over her shoulder.

Catty's name and address were hurriedly written on the back of the paper in Catty's handwriting. Above that was written in another person's penmanship, *in case of emergency contact my daughter*.

Kendra turned the paper over and over.

Catty knew it was her writing, but since when had she gotten an A in geometry? Then she saw the date on the test paper. It was a week away. Her heart started pounding rapidly.

A look of astonishment crossed Kendra's face as well, and she moved her thumb to cover the date. Kendra glanced at Catty, her mouth open in surprise.

"What?" Catty asked, wondering if Kendra had seen something more.

"Your moon amulet. It's changing colors." She seemed spellbound. "Maybe it is your mother," she suggested in a voice too low for the receptionist to hear. "Perhaps because you're close to your real mother, it's glowing." Kendra thought the amulet was a homing device that would someday guide Catty back to her home in space.

Catty clasped her hand around the amulet. It resonated against her palm. The amulet only glowed when Followers of the Atrox were nearby. Did that mean she was in danger? She looked quickly behind her, but nothing was there. She wished Vanessa were here.

Kendra's eyes widened and she put her hand on Catty's shoulder. Had she noticed something that Catty hadn't seen? Then Catty felt it. The air changed. She had a curious sensation of an electric charge building around her as if she had brushed a giant balloon vigorously back and forth across her clothing.

Overhead the fluorescent lights buzzed, then flickered, only to come back brighter.

"It must be a power surge," the receptionist offered in explanation, but Catty didn't think so.

The tiny hairs on her arm stood on end as if electrons were flowing through the air charging it with electricity, but that was impossible. A current of electricity needed a conductor and a source of energy. It couldn't just exist in the air. She might get Ds in geometry, but she always knew her science.

She touched Kendra's arm and a spark flew between them.

Kendra eyed her curiously. "What is it?" she whispered.

That's when the front entrance door opened

and three men walked slowly inside. They were distinguished-looking, with graying hair and deep, clear eyes. All three wore neatly pressed black suits.

When Kendra looked up and saw the men, she edged in front of Catty as if she were trying to protect her.

Catty peeked at the men from behind Kendra. The oldest had a thick mustache and held himself overly erect, as if he were wearing a brace. The shorter one had a broad, handsome face. He turned and smiled, his white, even teeth clenched tightly. When his black eyes met Catty's, she became suddenly aware of how frightened she felt. The third one seemed almost too good-looking. Catty wondered if he was wearing stage makeup. His skin and hair looked flaw-less.

If there hadn't been such a strange electrical aura surrounding them, and if her amulet hadn't been thrumming against her clenched fist, Catty might have thought they were undertakers from a mortuary that was patronized by only the rich and famous people in Los Angeles. But now she was certain the men were Followers, only different from any she had seen before. They were older, for one thing, and they looked too perfect, more like wax figures than real people.

Most of the Followers Catty met were Initiates. Kids who had turned to the Atrox, hoping to prove themselves worthy of becoming Followers. They were no threat to her, unless a large group of them caught her. But there were other Followers, like these, who were powerful and treacherous.

"I have to go," the receptionist announced. "Be sure to give the paper back before you leave."

The men turned to greet her as she walked back to the reception cubicle.

The oldest stepped forward. "We've come to claim the body of Zoe Reese," he said in a smooth voice.

Catty clutched Kendra's hand. Why would Followers want her mother's body?

The receptionist sighed. "Who notified *you?*"

"No one," he answered. "I am . . . *was* her neighbor. I called the police and informed them that I had found her body in the backyard. I knew she was alone in the world and I was hoping to make arrangements for her." He smiled coldly and leaned closer to the glass. "That is, of course, unless you were able to find a next of kin."

"The next of kin has already been notified." The receptionist glanced at Kendra and Catty but didn't say more.

"Perhaps, then . . ." He stopped and pressed a finger against his lips as if he were carefully considering his words before he continued. "Perhaps you could give me their address so that I might help them."

"I'm sorry," the receptionist answered solemnly. "I can't give you that information."

Kendra suddenly jerked Catty's arm and pulled her from the property release room. They marched quickly across the polished floor to the door and outside into the sunshine.

When they had passed two utility vans parked side by side, Kendra spoke quickly. "Don't look back until we're inside the car."

"You know who they are?" Catty felt surprised.

"They're from Area 51, I'm sure." Kendra quickened her pace. "That superclean military look. You'd think G-men would try to blend in rather than stand out. Did you see how polished their shoes were? That's not the first time I've had to hide you from their kind."

"Their kind?" Catty wondered if Kendra had seen Followers like these before.

"Government agents looking for space aliens," Kendra replied. The words came out in a single breath.

They climbed into the car and Kendra quickly rolled down her window. The air outside rushed in but did little to cool the interior.

"I've tried to protect you from government officials like those." Kendra sighed. "I'm sure they've taken others like you and dissected them. They'd just love to find out about your power.

Why do some scientists have this irrational need to dissect God's creatures? Can't they just admire their beauty?"

Catty shuddered. She wondered if some scientists really would dissect her in order to find out where her power came from.

Kendra started the car and turned on the air-conditioning.

"You've seen them before?" Catty asked nervously.

"Not for a long while. It was especially bad the day I found you on the desert . . ." Her words trailed away.

"They were there?" Catty didn't remember seeing them that day.

Kendra shook her head. "No, that night when we stopped in Yuma, the town was swarming with them. It was so obvious they were looking for you. That's why we didn't spend the night there but drove on to Palm Springs."

Catty remembered the night travel and how Kendra had sung songs to her, trying to keep her calm. She also remembered the strange way

Kendra had spoken to her at first, saying each word as if it contained three syllables and talking too loudly because she hadn't known if Catty understood English.

"You remember the day I picked you up at the side of the highway?" Kendra began and looked at Catty.

Catty nodded.

"You were such a precious little thing I couldn't imagine anyone abandoning you. I asked you your name, and you didn't seem to understand."

Catty recalled the moment. She had been unable to remember her name. Like everything that had occurred in her life before that day, she had no memory of it. She didn't even know if she had ever had one.

"When you didn't answer," Kendra continued, "I told you that you were as cute as a cat. That made you giggle, so I decided to call you Catty. You seemed to like the name."

Catty grinned. She did like the name.

Kendra smiled tenderly. "It was a good choice. It fits your personality." Then she glanced back at the building and continued her story. "I had planned to stop at the Department of Social Services in Yuma and turn you over to them, but then you did something extraordinary."

When Catty was little she had always encouraged Kendra to complete the story. "What made you think I was from outer space?" she would ask and cuddle closer. The story had both pleased and frightened her. She liked to think she had descended from some super race of creatures who traveled across galaxies, but at the same time she was afraid they might return and take her away from Kendra.

Kendra no longer needed coaxing to finish the story. "When we started to drive off, you grabbed my shoulder; and without warning, we were traveling through another dimension. It was like floating inside a dark endless tunnel, and then suddenly we were back on the road where I had picked you up, but now we were outside the car. I was terrified but I knew there had to be a rational explanation. That's when I decided you must come from another planet. I assumed that what we had done was some kind of teleportation."

Kendra never understood that Catty's gift was actually the ability to time-travel. Catty wondered what she would think if she knew.

"I figured that for a civilization that could travel across galaxies, the speed of light would be an archaic measure," Kendra went on. "So merely walking would probably seem as antiquated. I decided that when we went through that tunnel, you were actually trying to reconnect with your family. It made me feel so sad for you." She shook her head and stared at her hands. "Later when you told me about your memories of the crash and fire, I assumed that your spaceship had probably smashed into Earth, maybe killing your family and leaving you wandering on the desert."

Catty bit her lower lip. She should tell Kendra right now. "Kendra, there's something about me," she started, but then the three men left the coroner's office.

Kendra stared at them. "What do you think they were doing inside all this time?"

"Shouldn't we go?" Catty could feel her moon amulet pulsing against her chest and knew it was dangerous to stay.

Kendra put the car in reverse, but her movements were frustratingly slow as if she were debating whether to stay or leave.

Finally she spoke. "The woman must be your mother, Catty, and that's why the men are trying to claim her body without arousing suspicion. They can't afford another Roswell."

She squinted against the glaring sun, then remembered her sunglasses and brought them down from the top of her head to her nose. "We should have taken the envelope with the rest of her belongings. There might have been something important in it." Kendra pulled the geometry test from her purse and handed it to Catty.

Catty hadn't realized that Kendra had kept the paper until now.

"Government agents." Kendra spit out the words as if they left a bad taste in her mouth. "After all these years, they're back. You'll need to be careful, Catty. More careful than usual. I wonder if it's even safe for us to stay. Maybe we should leave Los Angeles."

Kendra's words left an uneasy foreboding in the air.

CHAPTER TWO

T HAT NIGHT, CATTY awakened with a start, her heart beating as if she had been running. She tried to bring the dream into focus, but the more she did, the more it seemed to slip away, leaving her with only a nagging feeling that there was something important she should be doing.

Moonlight streamed through the windows, giving her walls and furniture an eerie silver glow. Glancing at the butterfly chair next to her bed, she had the strangest impression that someone had been sitting in it, not just talking to her, but warning her about something. What had they said?

She rubbed her eyes. Her apprehension felt so real. It must mean something.

She tossed back her covers and rolled to the side of the bed. She tried to reassure herself that no one had been in the room. Her easel stood in the corner with her latest painting of a moonscape. The sketchpads and pencils on her desk looked the same as she had left them.

She listened to the silence for a long moment, then stood and walked to the chair. Her hand hovered above it. Finally, to convince herself that no one had been in the chair, she touched the seat. The faux-fur cover felt warm. She jerked her hand back as if it had been burned and scanned the room in disbelief. The warmth had to be stored heat, leftover from the day, but when she touched the edge of the chair, it felt cool.

Then she thought of Kendra and relaxed. How many nights had Kendra sat by her bed to comfort her? Kendra had probably come into her room to check on her, then sat down. Maybe she had even voiced her concerns about the "government men."

Catty took a deep breath and decided to go downstairs for a glass of milk.

In the hallway, the gray moonlight dissolved into total blackness. She waited until her eyes adjusted to the dark, then she continued to the stairs. She gripped the banister, and with quiet, even steps she made her way down to the living room.

At the entrance to the kitchen she stopped, suddenly aware of a cold draft. The back door was open and hanging on its hinges. Had an intruder come into the house? But why would a trespasser leave without shutting the door? Then she thought of Kendra upstairs and alone. Suddenly, she felt afraid for her. She rushed back through the dark house, stumbling up the stairs. Her breathing was hoarse by the time she opened the door to Kendra's room and switched on the light.

Kendra jerked awake and sat up in bed. "What's wrong?"

Catty walked slowly into the room. "I'm sorry to wake you." She slumped onto the bed and took deep breaths.

"What happened?" Kendra asked. "Are you all right?"

Catty shook her head. "I had this unbelievably crazy idea that you were in danger."

"I was," Kendra said softly.

"You were?" Catty looked quickly around the room. She didn't see anything that suggested danger.

"I was having one of those horrible nightmares." Kendra laughed softly, but the look in her eyes told Catty that the dream had truly frightened her. "You know the kind in which you can't wake up?"

Catty nodded. "What were you dreaming?"

"About those government men we saw in the coroner's office today." Kendra brushed her hands through her long hair and stretched.

"What were they doing?" Catty asked.

"They were chasing me because they wanted to find you." Kendra put her hand in front of her mouth to hide a yawn, then laughed. "They were demanding to see my memories, but I closed my mind to them." She shook her head. "I guess all that meditation makes me too focused," she joked. "Then they thought they could make me tell them where you were by force. It felt so real. One grabbed my arm and wouldn't let go. I'm glad you woke me."

Kendra must have seen something on Catty's face because she reached forward and patted Catty's cheek. "Don't be so concerned. It was only a dream."

When Catty didn't smile back at her, she continued. "Besides, the dream was probably only an expression of my very real fear that government officials *will* find you."

"Probably," Catty agreed, but secretly she wondered if these new Followers had a power she hadn't encountered before. Could they somehow go into dreams? Or was it only a strange coincidence that Kendra had dreamed about them? She grabbed Kendra's hand as if to protect her.

Kendra squeezed Catty's hand in return. "I love you, baby."

"I love you, too," Catty murmured.

Kendra got up and went to her bathroom,

splashed water on her face, then stared back at her raw-boned reflection in the mirror over the sink. Her eyes still held a charm, and her nose and cheekbones had an attractiveness, but nothing like the pictures that sat in the frames on her dresser.

Then Kendra looked down at her arm. "Odd."

"What?" Catty asked.

"Look at this." Kendra walked toward her, holding out her arm.

Catty stood and examined it. Four circular bruises colored the skin.

"I must have done this to myself while I was sleeping," Kendra announced, bemused.

Catty nodded. But she knew with a certainty that made her stomach curl that Kendra had not done that to herself. Somehow the Followers had found her in her dreams.

"Maybe I'll sleep in here for the rest of the night," Catty suggested.

"Okay," Kendra answered.

Catty knew from the quickness of her response that Kendra felt edgy about being alone.

She suddenly remembered the back door was still open.

"I'll get us some milk." Catty started to leave the bedroom. She didn't want to alarm Kendra about the open door. Besides, maybe the wind had blown it open.

"Good idea," Kendra called after her.

Catty hurried downstairs and closed the back door. As she slipped the dead bolt in place, she saw last year's Christmas pictures of Kendra's nieces and nephews on the refrigerator. She realized suddenly how much Kendra had sacrificed to protect her. Kendra rarely saw her family because she was afraid they might guess that Catty was a space alien. She also never dated for fear of exposing her. But Kendra never seemed to have any regrets for what she had had to give up to take care of Catty. Catty felt grateful, but also sad. Kendra loved her nieces and nephews and had always wanted a large family of her own. Catty hoped she wasn't going to repay her by putting her in danger.

CHAPTER THREE

THE DAY STARTED with a fire in the Sepulveda pass. By the time Catty walked to school, three new brushfires had begun burning in the hills surrounding Los Angeles. Newscasters blamed the continued drought and hot, dry weather. The air smelled of smoke, and gray ash drifted over La Brea High School.

Catty saw Vanessa leaning against the bank of lockers outside the classroom. She waved and hurried toward her. Like Catty, Vanessa had a special gift. She could expand her molecules and become invisible. But she didn't have complete control over it. If she became too upset or excited, her molecules acted on their own. That had made it difficult to date Michael at first, because every time he had tried to kiss her, she had started to go invisible. Catty wondered if she was having any trouble kissing Toby. Vanessa usually shared everything with her, but she had been closemouthed about him.

"Hi." Vanessa smiled. Her long blond hair shimmered in the morning sun.

"Hi," Catty answered and glanced down at Vanessa's flat, tanned stomach. White boxer shorts peeked over the top of her black, hip-hugging slacks. Catty wondered briefly if the boxers belonged to Toby.

Vanessa's blue eyes looked at Catty with concern. "Why weren't you at Planet Bang last night?"

Catty took in a deep breath. "It's a long story." She was glad Vanessa was no longer upset about what she had said yesterday.

"So tell me." Vanessa shifted her books.

"Hey." Jimena joined them. She was wearing a red tank top and jeans. Catty had tattooed the crescent moon and star on Jimena's arm. Jimena also had two teardrops tattooed under her eye. Her other tattoos, remnants from her gang days, were hidden under her clothes. She, too, had a gift. She received premonitions about the future.

Jimena glanced at Vanessa's outfit and playfully snapped the boxer's band. "Still trying to make Michael jealous?" she teased. "Or have you become somebody's *chavala*?"

"It's just a style," Vanessa huffed.

"Do the shorts belong to Toby?" Jimena smiled and brushed her luxurious black hair away from her face.

"So what if they do?" Vanessa muttered and looked away.

Jimena whooped. "I want to hear the whole story." But then she caught Catty's eyes, and her smile faded.

"It's just a style," Vanessa repeated, but Jimena didn't seem to hear her now, she was staring at Catty.

"What's wrong?" Jimena put a comforting

hand on Catty's shoulder. "Something big is bothering you. I don't need a premonition to know that, I can see it in your face."

Catty started to tell them about yesterday, when Serena ran up, carrying her cello case and geometry book.

"Hi, guys," she shouted. She was wearing a gold ring in her nose pierce. Her hair, curled and long, bounced on her shoulders. Serena and Jimena were best friends now, but their relationship had started uneasily. They hadn't become close until after they had fought a group of Followers together. That's when they had begun to trust each other.

Serena glanced at Vanessa and gave a loud laugh. "Are you wearing Toby's underwear?"

Vanessa looked around quickly. "Do you want everyone to hear?"

Serena set down her cello case. "It's only natural—people are going to talk."

Vanessa blushed.

"Come on, I'm kidding!" Serena said. "So

why is everyone so quiet?" Then she glanced at Catty. "What's wrong?"

Catty started to speak but couldn't find the words at first. "I'm not even sure where to begin."

They gathered close around her.

Catty rubbed her forehead and slowly began to tell them everything that had happened the day before at the coroner's office.

"Why do you think Followers would come to the coroner's office to claim my mother's body?" she asked finally.

"Maybe it's just another group of Followers we have to deal with and it has nothing to do with your mother," Serena suggested.

"Yeah," Vanessa agreed. "If they knew about your mother, maybe they went there hoping to catch you off guard."

Catty shuddered. "I hope they never get me again."

Jimena continued. "Remember what Maggie told us? Ambitious Followers come to Los Angeles because the Daughters of the Moon live here."

"We're the biggest prize," Serena added. "If they get one of us, the Atrox rewards them by allowing them into the Inner Circle."

Catty nodded but she still wondered if her mother had had some kind of association with these Followers.

"They didn't seem like ordinary Followers," Catty continued slowly. "They were old, for one thing, and then they had this high-voltage aura."

"You mean there was an evil feeling in the room?" Vanessa asked.

Catty shook her head. "No, the room felt like . . ." She thought for a moment. "You know when you brush your hand in front of the TV or the screen on your computer monitor?"

They nodded.

"Like that," Catty explained. "The air felt fuzzy as if it were filled with static electricity."

She sensed Serena entering her mind to try and get a better understanding of what she was saying. Like the rest of them, Serena hadn't understood her power when she was little. She only knew then that she was different. Sometimes, she forgot that people weren't speaking aloud and she would answer their thoughts. She did it even now if she became too happy or excited.

Catty looked at her three best friends. Maggie had brought them all together and was still showing them how to use their special powers to fight the Atrox and its Followers. She called them an unstoppable force, but more often they felt as if their powers controlled them. Of all the Daughters, Catty had the strangest power. She missed a lot of school because she was always twisting time. Vanessa was the only one who had time-traveled with Catty so far.

A few moments later, Serena left Catty's mind and stared at her. "Freaky."

"There's more," Catty added.

"What?" Vanessa asked.

"The receptionist in the coroner's office gave us this from my mother's belongings." Catty pulled out the wrinkled and worn geometry test.

Jimena took it. Vanessa and Serena studied it over her shoulder.

"Look at the date," Serena whispered.

"Wow," Vanessa breathed.

"But we don't have a test scheduled for next week, do we?" Jimena asked.

"No," Vanessa said.

"You've never gotten an A in geometry before," Serena teased.

Catty rolled her eyes. "I know."

Vanessa seemed puzzled. "How could your mother get something from the future if she's already dead?"

"Weird," Serena commented.

"Did you get the rest of your mother's things?" Jimena asked.

Catty shook her head.

"Maybe if you could have looked through all of her things, you'd have some answers," Vanessa suggested. "There could be something important that you missed."

"Yeah, some clue," Jimena agreed.

"Maybe we should ask Stanton," Serena put in. "I'm sure he'd know about these new Followers."

The others turned and stared at her.

"Well, he might," Serena answered defensively.

Catty knew Serena wanted an excuse to find Stanton. She still liked him, even though she tried to act like she didn't. Stanton was a powerful Follower who could read minds, manipulate thoughts, and even imprison people in his memories. Serena had fallen in love with him. She didn't think he was evil, but Catty had never gotten used to Serena being with a Follower. She didn't trust Stanton and thought Serena was putting them all in danger by seeing him. Then unexpectedly Stanton had ended their relationship. He had told her it was too dangerous, because if the Atrox found out about them, it would send Regulators to destroy them. Serena thought that proved how much Stanton cared for her, but Catty wondered if it was only another trick to gain even more of her trust.

"So why is everyone being so quiet?" Serena looked from one to the other suspiciously as if she knew they were feeling sorry for her.

"It's not a good idea," Catty answered bluntly.

"It's dangerous for you to hang around with Stanton."

Serena started to say something back, but Vanessa interrupted her. "Mr. Hall is coming."

Mr. Hall swung on old leather briefcase in one hand and jangled his keys in the other. He shaved his head, wore tiny black-rimmed glasses and had a beak nose that he was always wiping with his handkerchief.

"So everyone be extra careful until we can see Maggie," Vanessa warned. "Especially you, Catty. Promise?"

Catty nodded.

Vanessa gave her a worried look. "I mean, *really* promise."

Catty looked at her. "Why?"

"Because you always go off on your own even when it's dangerous," Vanessa complained.

"That's true," Serena agreed.

I do not, Catty started to say. But she knew they were right. "Okay, I promise."

Mr. Hall unlocked the classroom door, and

the girls followed him inside and took their seats.

He set his briefcase on the desk, then took a piece of chalk and wrote a date on the blackboard. He pulled a handkerchief from his back pocket and swiped it under his nose as he clicked the chalk against the board. "Next week we'll have a midterm," he announced.

Catty glanced down at the worn geometry test paper. The date on the paper matched the date on the blackboard.

She turned and looked at Vanessa. Her eyes were wide with astonishment.

"The same date," Jimena whispered with surprise.

"What do you suppose it means?" Serena asked.

"Girls," Mr. Hall cautioned.

Catty stared down at the paper. Her heart pounded rapidly. She wondered if maybe she would finally be able to go back in time to the day when Kendra had found her walking along the highway. So far when she had tried to go back to that day, she had become stuck in the tunnel. It was a horrible claustrophobic sensation; floating for hours in the black void before she was able to free herself. But she kept risking it, because more than anything, she wanted to see her mother.

FTER CLASS, CATTY threw her geometry book into her locker. She was about to pick up her Spanish book when someone ran down the hallway and grabbed her waist. She twirled around. Chris stood behind her. He was a good-looking guy with an adorable smile and spiky hair. He wore bagged-out jeans and his red leather Reeboks.

She stared into his clear eyes and wondered how she could like him so much.

"I've been trying to find you since last night. You weren't at Planet Bang." He pulled her closer, and she let him. She liked the feel of his body next to hers.

"Things came up." Another time she might have told him everything, but since yesterday, she felt guarded.

"Missed you," he confessed.

She felt a smile crawl uninvited across her face. She didn't want him to see how much she cared for him.

"A guy in the school band is having a party," he announced.

She loved the way a smile made his eyes shine.

"I was hoping you'd go with me," he continued.

She felt a thrill of excitement and almost said yes, but at that moment he glanced down the hallway as if suddenly worried that someone might see them together. Then he slammed her locker and pulled Catty around the corner, his eyes drifting over her head as he scanned the crowd of kids walking down the corridor behind them.

"Who are you looking for?" she asked.

A light blush rose under his tanned cheeks, and his eyes shot back to hers. "Looking? What do you mean?"

"Your eyes keep wandering," she accused him.

"No they don't," he argued.

"Yeah." She nodded. "Like you're afraid someone is going to catch us together."

He laughed it off, but she wasn't convinced. She'd heard about guys who tried to have three and four girlfriends at a time, like it was some kind of sport, but Chris didn't seem like that kind of guy. Still, the way he was acting made her wonder. Then another thought came to her. He had just transferred to La Brea High, so it was also possible that he still had a girlfriend at his old school. Maybe someone here knew his old girlfriend, and he didn't want that person seeing him with Catty.

"Do you have a girlfriend?" she asked boldly. She tilted her head and watched his eyes closely.

"No." His eyes remained steady on hers, and she believed him. Then he touched her cheek, and a sweet shock of delight rushed through her. "Why would you think that?"

"Just wondering," she answered.

He smiled and she began to relax. How could she ever think such things about Chris?

"It's going to be a great party," he coaxed. "Lots of garage bands are going to play, and everyone is going to be there."

She started to say yes, but then his eyes left hers again.

"I don't know," Catty muttered.

He glanced back, and she hated the wounded look on his face. She wanted to tell him yes, but first she needed to find out what was going on.

"Why not?" he asked. "You know we'll have a good time. We always have a great time to-gether."

"Chris, there's something I've been wanting to talk to you about since yesterday."

"Sure." He took her hand. She loved the feel of his hand, holding hers. Was there another girl who felt the same way? "Tell me," he encouraged her.

"You've seemed . . ." She stumbled, trying to find the right words. She decided to just say it. "You've changed." She caught something in his eyes then, a sudden nervousness. So he *had* been acting different, and he was also aware of it. "Is something wrong between us?"

"No, everything's fine." She sensed a lie in his words.

"Tell me the truth," she said matter-of-factly. "I thought we always shared everything."

His lips started to move, but before he could say anything, Jimena, Serena, and Vanessa ran up to them.

Jimena spoke first, and there was real concern in her voice. "You disappeared so quickly, we were afraid something had happened."

"What could happen at school?" Chris asked with a smile.

"Things." Vanessa looked at Catty. "One minute you're at your locker, the next you're gone."

"I pulled Catty away," Chris answered. "Sorry, I didn't know it would cause such a big commotion."

Serena cocked her head to the side and tried to smile but her tongue pierce clicked nervously against her teeth. "We just thought maybe someone had kidnapped her," she joked, but Catty knew they were worried that the new Followers might have captured her.

Chris smiled. "I was just asking her to a party one of the guys who plays in the school band is having," he explained. "You guys want to come, too?"

"Sure," Jimena answered quickly.

"It could take our mind off other things." Serena looked pointedly at Catty.

"Yeah." Vanessa seemed really eager. "I can't wait to show off all the new dance sequences I've learned with Toby."

Catty was surprised. That was so unlike Vanessa. She used to be nervous about dancing.

"Well?" Chris looked at Catty. "What do you say?"

"All right, I'll go." Catty sighed. She wasn't sure she was doing the right thing.

"Great." Chris kissed her cheek. "See ya." He

darted away toward the music room for band practice. He played tuba in the marching band.

"What's up with Chris?" Jimena asked.

"Yeah," Serena added. "I thought you liked him."

Catty sighed. "I did—I mean I really do like him a lot, but he's acting so . . ." She shrugged. "I just get the feeling that he's seeing someone else. Whenever we're together, he's always looking over my shoulder like he doesn't want anyone to see us together."

"No way," Jimena disagreed. "He's such a sweet guy."

"He's really cool and funny, too," Serena added.

"You worry too much," Vanessa offered. "Besides maybe it's other things. Maybe you've been acting weird and it makes him feel unsure."

"Me?" Catty said in disbelief.

"It's not like you don't have a lot going on," Serena declared. "You said yourself that yesterday was the worst day of your life."

"De veras," Jimena agreed.

Catty nodded and considered what they were saying. She didn't think her problems were making her believe Chris was seeing someone else. Besides, she knew him well enough to know something was going on.

The bell rang.

"I can't be late again," Serena complained.

"Come on," Jimena yelled.

Serena and Jimena ran down the hallway. Vanessa started after them, but Catty grabbed her arm and held her back.

Vanessa looked at her curiously. "What? I'm going to be late."

"I'm sorry," Catty cut in. "But I need to talk to you."

"Can't it wait?" Vanessa asked and started edging away. "You know how much I hate to be late for class."

Catty shook her head.

Vanessa seemed suddenly worried and stepped back to Catty. "What is it?"

"I want you to go back in time with me," Catty pleaded.

"No," Vanessa answered firmly and started to walk away.

Catty clasped her hand and pulled her close. "Please—I know you hate it, but I want to go back to the coroner's office and get my mother's things."

Vanessa shook her head.

"You're the one who said I should have looked through all of her stuff," Catty reminded her. "I might have missed something important that could give me answers."

"But you don't need me for that," Vanessa argued. "I'd just be in the way."

"The Followers will be there."

"Go back earlier before they get there," Vanessa suggested. "You'll be safe then."

"The property release room won't be open yet." Catty stared intently into Vanessa's eyes, hoping to see some sign that she was relenting.

"So? Go back and land inside the property release room," Vanessa advised.

"My landings have never been that accurate,"

Catty pointed out. "You say that all the time."

"Just call them up then." There was rising impatience in Vanessa's voice. "They have to release her things to you. Kendra can help you."

"That could take months," Catty answered. "And what if Kendra and I take the forms in or do whatever we have to do and the Followers are waiting for us to show up again? I could get kidnapped."

"Going back now is just as risky," Vanessa argued.

"You made me promise not to go off and do anything on my own." Catty folded her arms across her chest. "But I guess I'll have to."

Vanessa's eyes widened. "It's too dangerous."

Catty knew she had her now. "Not if you make us invisible so we can sneak past the Followers and the receptionist and steal my mother's things from the property room."

"I'm sure it's against the law," Vanessa objected. "Can't you do it the right way for once?"

"I already explained why I can't," Catty told her. "Besides, it's not like we'd really be stealing anything. Whatever is in the envelope belonged to my mother and should go to me. Think how you'd feel."

"All right," Vanessa agreed reluctantly.

"Great!" Catty grabbed her hand.

"But not here," Vanessa complained. "Someone might see us."

"All right." But it was too late. Catty could feel the power surging in her mind and pressing outward against her skull.

Vanessa had an astonished look on her face. She knew what was happening.

Catty glanced down. The hands on her watch began turning backward, and an abnormal heaviness crackled through the air. Vanessa shrieked and dropped her books as the school roared away with a burst of white light. Sucked into the tunnel that opened behind them, they whirled downward in air that felt dry and at the same time seemed to feel fizzy and effervescent.

Vanessa choked and coughed. She could

barely breathe in the thick foul air. Catty had gotten used to it.

She glanced down at her watch.

"Now!" she shouted in warning. Vanessa also hated the landings.

They fell back into time. In her mind's eye, Catty saw herself landing softly on two feet, but instead she fell and skidded across the parking lot in front of the coroner's office. Her chin hit the ground with a sharp crack. "Ow!"

Vanessa landed next to her.

"Sorry," Catty muttered and stood, brushing off her clothes.

Vanessa shook her head. "That one was worse than normal."

Catty stared at the building. "I know," she confessed, rubbing her chin. "I'm nervous."

A horn honked. Catty turned. A car was coming slowly toward them.

"Yikes," Vanessa said and grabbed Catty's hand. "We're in the middle of the parking lot. I hope no one saw us land."

"Too late now," Catty commented.

They dove between two utility vans parked side by side.

Catty started laughing. "Can you imagine what the driver must have thought if he saw us falling from the air?"

"How would we have explained ourselves?" Vanessa asked, but then she started laughing, too. "Hello, sir, we were just dropping from the sky."

Finally, Catty stopped laughing and turned to Vanessa. "Ready?"

"Okay." Vanessa stared at the two buildings connected by a broad cement walkway. She seemed more apprehensive than usual. "Which building do we go into?"

Catty pointed. "That one."

Vanessa read the words on the side of the building. *"Department of Coroner. Medical Examiner. Forensic Laboratories."* She shuddered. "Is that where they keep . . ." Vanessa stopped, then started again. "Is that where they keep the bodies?"

Catty looked at her. "In the basement. We don't have to go down there."

Vanessa took in a deep breath. "All right

then, but it still creeps me out."

"Let's get it over with," Catty urged.

Vanessa grabbed Catty tightly around her waist and pulled her close. Catty breathed through her lips trying to suppress her nervousness. Almost immediately her molecules began to stir and a pleasant ache spread through her body. She glanced down at her hands and watched in amazement as skin, muscle, and bone began to separate into innumerable specks. In a few seconds she was able to see through her hand. Finally there was nothing to look at, only air.

They caught a breeze and drifted toward the coroner's office.

Catty didn't glance back. She was afraid if she did she might see Kendra and herself sitting in the car staring back at the building.

There was a large crack between the two glass doors, and Vanessa sifted through it, taking Catty with her. If Catty had been able to scream, she would have. She wondered how Vanessa could be so afraid of the tunnel. Being invisible was far spookier.

Inside, the cool air seeped through them. The cold was bad, but worse was the electrical charge that hovered around the three Followers standing near the reception window.

Vanessa paused. Catty pushed her molecules in the direction of the property release door and they started floating that way.

Then Catty sensed something odd. What was happening? She experienced a sharp pain like a pinprick, quickly followed by another and another. Her molecules were colliding. She glanced where she thought her hands would be and saw a mass of dots. Was she becoming visible? She looked nervously at Vanessa. Her face was forming.

"Oops," Vanessa mouthed.

Catty's molecules clashed together with an abruptness that left her skin tingling. She fell to the floor and landed on top of Vanessa.

"What happened?" she whispered.

"Sorry," Vanessa answered. "I got so spooked thinking about all the dead people in here that I lost control."

"That's the least of our problems." Catty

glanced up as the Followers turned languidly and stared down at them.

"Do they know who we are?" Vanessa asked.

"Let's not take any chances." Catty scrambled to her feet and bolted for the door, dragging Vanessa with her. But before she could reach it the Follower with the broad face stepped in front of her and blocked her way.

"Is there a problem?" he spoke in a polite voice.

"No, none at all," Catty answered with a nervous smile as Vanessa tugged her arm and pulled her in the opposite direction.

They dodged around the other two Followers and ran down the hallway, past a sign that read ATTENTION VISITORS, LAW ENFORCEMENT ID BADGE MUST BE WORN BEYOND THIS POINT.

"I think we're trespassing," Vanessa said. "I swear, Catty, someday you're going to get me arrested."

"Not as long as I can change time," Catty smirked.

Their feet pounded heavily on the floor.

"You can't go down there!" the receptionist yelled after them.

Catty and Vanessa darted around a corner and pressed against a door.

"You hide," Vanessa ordered.

"Me?" Catty peered back down the hallway. The Followers were coming at a slow even pace. "Why not both of us?"

"I'll let the Followers chase after me, then I'll go invisible so they'll lose my trail and you'll have time to find what you're looking for."

"I don't know." Catty felt reluctant to leave her. "It could be dangerous. Maybe it's better if we stay together and try to fight them."

The plodding footsteps of the Followers grew steadily louder.

"Just do it. We'll meet in the basement," Vanessa called over her shoulder as she started to run.

Catty slipped into a utility room behind her and watched through a crack in the door as the three men followed Vanessa.

When they passed, she started to leave the

room but other footfalls made her pause.

The receptionist and a security guard hurried down the corridor. After they went by, Catty eased back into the hallway. She had promised to meet Vanessa in the basement, but there was something she had to do first.

She crept back to the property-release room. The door was still open. She peeked inside. The clerk was humming, her back to Catty.

The brown envelope with her mother's belongings sat on a small file cabinet. She held her breath and tiptoed forward. Glancing up, she saw her reflection in the huge convex mirror that hung in the corner like a giant bug eye. If the woman looked up, she would see her.

Catty steadied herself and took another step forward. She picked up the envelope. The paper crinkled and something inside moved across the bottom.

The clerk stopped humming and cocked her head, listening, then hunched back over a pile of papers and began ruffling through them.

Catty turned and started silently back to the

door. She had only gone a little way, when she heard footsteps behind her.

She glanced back. The clerk was walking toward her. Catty's heart pounded so loudly she was sure the clerk could hear it.

"You still here?" the clerk questioned. It was the same woman from yesterday. "I thought you'd left." She didn't seem to notice that Catty was wearing different clothes.

Catty nodded.

"Did you put the paper back in the envelope?" She looked at the envelope in Catty's hands.

"The receptionist still has it," Catty lied.

"Make sure she brings it back," she ordered.

"Yes, ma'am."

The clerk inclined her head and studied Catty briefly, then satisfied, she returned to the pile of papers she had been sorting in the corner.

Catty left the room. The reception area was still empty. She turned, hurried down the hallway, and found an elevator. She pressed the button impatiently. The metal doors slowly scraped open. She rushed in and immediately pushed another button. When the doors finally closed, she let out a long sigh of relief.

As the elevator trundled down, she opened the envelope and peered inside.

She lifted out a chain and held it up. Her breath caught. Dangling from the end was a moon amulet that matched her own, except for the odd coloring. It looked tarnished and blackened as if it had been in a fire. She studied the face of the moon etched in the metal. Had her mother been a Daughter of the Moon?

THE ELEVATOR DOORS opened with a rasping sound, and Catty peeked out at the hallway. When she didn't see anyone, she took a cautious step forward, stopped, and listened. Overhead the fluorescent lights buzzed, then dimmed and lit again as if there had been a power surge. She glanced up and wondered if the Followers had caused it.

"Vanessa?" she called tentatively and slipped her mother's moon amulet into her pocket. She tossed the envelope into a tall white trash cylinder.

◄ 6 7 ►

She took a few more steps when the lights flickered and went out. She stood in complete darkness before the emergency lighting came on behind her. Slowly her eyes became accustomed to the dim light and she started again.

As she passed the numbered rooms, she drew in a deep long breath and immediately regretted it. The smell was too antiseptic. Her stomach felt suddenly queasy.

"Where are you, Vanessa?" she called softly.

She looked at the long line of doors in front of her and wondered what she would see if she ventured into one of the rooms. She tried not to think about it and crept farther down the hallway.

The door to the next room was partly open. She tiptoed past it.

The utter silence seemed too deep and unnatural but then, she reasoned, if the electricity had gone off, there would be no sounds from air conditioners or buzzing lights that normally filled any large office building.

She stepped into the heavy shadow near an open door and wished that Vanessa would hurry.

"Where is she?" she whispered with rising anxiety.

A sound from behind her made her alert. She took an uncertain step into the deeper shadows inside the room.

"Vanessa!" She tried again. "Now's not the time to play games."

Silence answered her.

"That's it. I'm leaving."

She started to turn to go back to the elevator when a hand reached out from behind her and touched her shoulder.

CHAPTER SIX

A LONG HISS OF AIR escaped Catty's lungs. She stood motionless, waiting for the person to speak. When they didn't she rushed to give an explanation. "I'm sorry," she said, assuming the person was a security guard. "I took the elevator, then the lights went out and I got lost."

The person didn't answer.

She tried to turn her head to see who stood behind her, but when she did a gloved hand stopped her.

"What?" Catty whispered nervously.

"Don't turn," the person whispered. The

voice was magnetic, and it was definitely a guy. It also seemed familiar.

"Who are you?" she asked, still trying to identify the voice.

"Catty." He spoke her name quietly.

A shock ran through her. "Yes," she answered with a quiver in her voice. "How do you know my name? Do I know you?"

"I have something for you," he said, ignoring her questions.

There was a rustling behind her and then the gloved hand reached over her shoulder and gave her something that looked like a thick piece of paper.

She took it and recognized the feel of parchment. She held it close to her eyes. It was a lavishly decorated medieval manuscript or something that looked like one. The first letters caught the light from the hallway and sparkled in gold. Strange birds and exotic animals hidden in a tangle of foliage and fairy-tale landscapes lined the borders.

"You're giving this to me?" Catty asked. If it

were authentic it would be priceless. "Is it stolen?"

There was a pause, followed by a chuckle. "It belongs to you."

"Me?" She smoothed her hand over the swirling script.

"Take the manuscript and use it," he instructed.

"Use it how?"

"The manuscript contains the answers to your questions."

She wondered who he was. She wanted to turn and see his face but every time she tried, his hand would stop her again.

"I don't understand," she murmured at last. "What questions should I have?"

He paused for a long moment.

"Read the manuscript," he answered. "Then you will know."

"Know what?" Catty asked. "What am I supposed to know?"

She could feel him take a step away from her.

"Don't try to follow me," he warned.

"Please don't go, not yet," she pleaded. She wanted to find out more about him.

She hadn't even realized he had left until she heard his footsteps echoing down the hallway behind her.

She stood motionless, staring at the manuscript. Should she follow him? He had said not to, but she didn't understand why. A devious smile crossed her face. She had always hated rules. She turned suddenly and ran to the doorway. She didn't see him in the long deserted corridor, but he had to be someplace nearby. She hurried in the way he had gone, her feet slapping loudly. She glanced at the closed doors, wondering where he had hidden.

Ahead of her a door was open. She stopped and peeked cautiously inside. It looked like a huge storage room. She took two stealthy steps inside. The shadows seemed deep and foreboding. She didn't even want to consider what was resting on the gurney, wrapped in plastic.

A harsh voice spoke behind her. "You must never try to discover who I am, do you understand?"

She nodded.

"That is essential," he warned. "Your very existence could depend on it, Catty." He spoke her name with tenderness as if he had known her for a long time. "Do you understand?"

"Why?" she asked in a hushed tone. "Why should knowing you put me in danger?"

"Simply accept that it is true."

She believed him but she wanted to know why. Before she could ask again, his gloved hand took her hand. She tried to see him from the corner of her eyes, but darkness kept him hidden.

"Trust me," he whispered.

"Yes," she answered. "I trust you." And at the same time she wondered how she could trust a complete stranger.

"Good-bye." He spoke the word against the side of her neck and it sent a pleasing shiver down her back.

Now more than anything she wanted to know who he was. She turned abruptly, expecting to be face-to-face with him. But the room was empty.

Suddenly she heard footsteps echoing in the corridor. Excitement rushed through her. If he were in the corridor, she would have enough light to see who he was.

She ran out the door and collided into Vanessa.

"There you are." Vanessa sounded angry. "How could you leave me alone in this place for so long? I'd rather face the Followers than creep around these passageways."

Catty started to show Vanessa the manuscript, but a noise made her stop.

At the end of the hallway, two Followers pushed open a large metal door and stepped from the stairwell.

They turned and started walking toward Vanessa and Catty. The air took on an odd fuzziness, and Catty could feel the hairs on the back of her neck rise as static electricity whisked around them.

"Why are there only two?" Vanessa asked nervously. "What happened to the third one?"

Catty shook her head. "I don't know."

"Take us back, Catty," Vanessa urged. She clutched Catty's hand. "Hurry."

"I can't," Catty answered, feeling too flustered to attempt opening the tunnel. "Can't you make us invisible?"

"Are you kidding? I can barely breathe."

"We better try to fight them off." Catty braced herself. "That takes less energy."

Catty and Vanessa stood together, concentrated, and sent their mental energy spiraling at the Followers. The hallway filled with a gleaming light. Catty felt the power rise up in her, but the Followers didn't stop their slow steady advance and they didn't respond with an attack of their own. Instead, they smiled at Catty and Vanessa as if they found their efforts amusing.

"What's with them?" Catty asked. Her nerves were raw, but nothing was happening.

"Take us back to the present," Vanessa urged. "This is getting too totally spooky."

"I'll try." Catty took Vanessa's hand but her energy felt drained. She couldn't concentrate. "I don't think I can. I don't have enough power right now."

"You have to. Hurry!"

Catty struggled to open the tunnel. "I can't. But I've got a plan."

"What?"

Catty grabbed Vanessa's hand. "Run!"

They turned and ran down the corridor as the third Follower suddenly appeared at that end and began walking toward them.

Vanessa clasped Catty's hand. "Please, Catty, now. Just try."

Catty clutched the manuscript tightly against her chest and squeezed her eyes shut. Nothing happened.

The Followers pressed closer.

"Never again," Vanessa whimpered. "I am never doing this again."

"You're being optimistic," Catty tried to joke in spite of her rising fear. "You think we get another chance?"

The Follower with the thick mustache reached out to touch Catty. A flurry of blue

sparks shot in the air like miniature forked lightning bolts.

"I'm sorry, Vanessa," Catty sighed. "So
sorry."

CHAPTER SEVEN

ABRUPTLY, VANESSA wrapped her arms around Catty.

"Relax," she ordered.

"Right."

Catty's molecules began spreading outward, and she watched in wonder as her body started to dissolve. Instantly Catty and Vanessa were both invisible, rising above the hallway. They drifted over the heads of the Followers, and continued in an easy flow up the stairwell, through the brightly polished upstairs corridors and then out into the hot afternoon.

Vanessa didn't make them visible again until they were in the back of the building near the freeway, then they became whole. Catty tumbled to the ground.

"Can you take us back now?" Vanessa seemed nervous and tired.

"Sure." Catty stood slowly and smoothed her hands down her body. Her skin still prickled and she felt shaky. She had almost forgotten the manuscript. She picked it off the ground. "How did you make us invisible?"

"It doesn't matter," Vanessa grumbled.

"Tell me." Catty offered Vanessa a hand and pulled her up.

"Okay, but it doesn't mean anything." Vanessa hesitated a moment. "I thought of Michael."

"What?" Catty smirked. "I thought you were through with him."

"I told you it doesn't mean anything," Vanessa argued, but Catty wondered if she was just trying to convince herself. "Just take us back, okay?"

Catty nodded and concentrated. She held the manuscript in one hand and Vanessa's hand in the other. She could feel her power growing. At once the hot afternoon burst away and they were falling into cool blackness. It took a few seconds for Catty's eyes to adjust and by then it was time to fall back into the present. They landed in Catty's backyard.

Catty glanced at her watch. "Sorry. School's over. I hope you didn't have anything important today."

Vanessa lay in the grass with her arms spread. "I don't care right now. I've never been so grateful to be back in the present," she paused. "Those Followers were the creepiest we've ever come across. Why didn't our powers work against them?"

Catty waved the manuscript over her.

Vanessa blinked. "What's that?" She stood and brushed her hands through her hair.

"Come inside, and I'll show you." Catty started across the patio. She opened the sliding glass door and they stepped into the kitchen.

Catty set the manuscript in the middle of the kitchen table. She and Vanessa leaned over it and studied the rich illuminated borders, the enlarged first letter ornamented with interlaced patterns in gold, red, and blue and the detailed miniature within the first letter of someone locking the jaws of hell. The figure looked like a goddess, but there was something disturbing about her eyes. They looked phosphorescent, like the eyes of a Follower in moonlight.

"What does it say?" Vanessa wondered.

Catty ran her finger along the words and tried to translate the Latin. When she couldn't, she looked at Vanessa. "I don't get it. We can speak and understand Latin, so why can't I read it?"

Vanessa pointed to the framed medieval manuscript page that hung on the wall between two of Catty's watercolors. It was Kendra's prized possession. Even though it wasn't a valuable piece, Kendra loved the old Latin script.

"Remember what Kendra said? Old Latin manuscripts are difficult to translate even for scholars because the scribes had their own personal quirks and distinct way of writing, and different regions had their own types of script."

Catty remembered how Kendra became frustrated with the translations until she could get used to each scribe's individual style. But that was also what Kendra liked about translating the old documents; she felt as if she got to know the scribe's personality after studying his work. "I guess it's no wonder I can't read it."

"Hey, maybe Kendra will do it for us," Vanessa suggested.

"Kendra will do what for you?" Kendra walked into the kitchen, holding a pile of newspapers. She dumped them in the paper recycle bin. She was wearing a black sports bra and leggings.

Catty glanced up, happy to see her. On Wednesdays she always closed the shop early. Catty held up the manuscript. "Maybe you can translate this for us."

Kendra took the reading glasses hanging from the chain around her neck, slipped them on, and studied the manuscript. She was awestruck. "How did you get such a priceless piece of work?"

Catty told her about the mysterious stranger. Both Kendra and Vanessa were spellbound. When she finished, Kendra studied the manuscript again.

"This is highly unusual." She took off her reading glasses and tapped them gently in the palm of her hand. "So often in medieval pieces the scribe's work is mechanical, typical of the armies of transcribers who didn't know Latin, but labored in the scriptoriums copying books word by word, letter by letter onto the parchment. But this manuscript is different. I think it might even be older than that."

"What do you mean?" Catty asked.

"There's a fluidity in the lettering at the beginning, but then toward the end, the writing looks more rushed."

"Does it mention the moon?" Vanessa asked.

Kendra nodded. "Yes it does, and it also mentions a curse."

Catty and Vanessa stared at each other. "A curse?" they said together.

Kendra nodded. "There's a curse for anyone who holds the manuscript." She put her reading glasses back on, then looked down and translated the warning. *"To hold the manuscript is to capture misery and death."*

She continued translating the first line. *"The Atrox arose from primal darkness."* She stopped and looked back at Catty and Vanessa. "What in the world is an Atrox?"

Vanessa and Catty exchanged frightened looks. Had the mystery man actually given her something dangerous?

"Atrox," Kendra repeated. "It's probably one of the scribe's little quirks. Some word he either misspells or doesn't know." She glanced at the clock. "Time for my yoga. Will you excuse me?" No matter what was going on, Kendra always stopped for her yoga and meditation. It could be frustrating at times.

Catty waited until she heard Kendra rolling out her mats in the living room, then she turned to Vanessa. "I think we better call Serena and Jimena and take the manuscript to Maggie tomorrow."

Vanessa nodded in agreement.

CHAPTER EIGHT

T

HE NEXT DAY after school, Catty crawled into the backseat of Jimena's brother's car. Jimena didn't have her driver's license yet but when her brother visited from San Diego, he let her use his '81 Oldsmobile. She had learned how to drive when she was in a gang and jacking cars.

"Why are we going to Westwood?" Catty asked.

"Not Westwood," Serena corrected from the passenger seat. "The Federal Building."

Jimena gripped the steering wheel. "Maggie's taking part in a demonstration," she answered as she pulled away from the curb with a squeal of rubber.

"Yeah," Serena winked. "She said she'd be in the crowd. Just find her."

"What do you suppose she's protesting?" Vanessa wondered.

Jimena zipped the car into the traffic on Doheny. The muffler rumbled against the street with a deep throaty sound that Catty liked.

"They protest everything there," Catty put in. "It's like a party. Kendra says it's a great place to meet people."

"Maybe Maggie's getting lonely and wants to meet some guy," Jimena added with a wry smile.

Serena shook her head. "Maggie's upset that the tuna industry is still harming dolphins."

Jimena eyed Catty in the rearview mirror. "Did you bring the manuscript?"

Catty nodded. "It's in my messenger bag."

"I can't believe we're treating a priceless manuscript like that." Vanessa shook her head.

"We don't know that it's worth anything to anyone but the Atrox." Catty pulled off her sunglasses and then she noticed something different about Vanessa. "You're not wearing your moon amulet."

Serena and Jimena both turned to look at Vanessa. Jimena's eyes shifted back to the road. She buzzed around a bus, then made a sweeping left-hand turn.

Vanessa rubbed a rough patch of red skin on her chest. "It was giving me a rash. Mom said it probably wasn't the amulet but some cream that reacted with the metal."

"You never take it off." Catty looked at her curiously.

Vanessa stared out the window as if she didn't want to continue the conversation. "I know, but I couldn't stand the itching."

Jimena parked in the lot behind the Federal Building. The girls climbed out, and walked toward Wilshire Boulevard. Sunlight filtered through the smoky sky and cast a surreal orange glow across the hot afternoon.

A gathering of people lined the street protesting global warming, abortion, animal rights, and INS violations. A smaller group stood at the edge of the curb, waving placards at passing motorists. Maggie twirled a sign that read SAVE THE DOLPHINS. She was a thin short woman with long gray hair curled into a bun on top of her head. She wore dangling earrings, a flowing orange and purple dress, and a large canvas bag hung from her shoulder. Her temples were beaded with perspiration.

The girls approached her and she hugged each in turn. A man with a full beard stood next to her. He set down his sign and nodded at the girls in greeting.

"You have lovely granddaughters, Maggie." He extended his hand to Catty. "I'm George."

"George is a dear old friend." Maggie looked at him with warm caring eyes. "You'll excuse us for a moment, George?" She handed him her placard and he went back to the curb, holding both signs high in the air.

Maggie threaded through the other protesters. The girls followed after her.

Finally she stopped in the shade near the

building. A security guard eyed them suspiciously.

"Now, my dears, what is going on?" Maggie took a Kleenex from her pocket and patted it across her forehead.

Catty opened her messenger bag and handed the manuscript to Maggie.

Maggie touched the brittle parchment reverentially. "The Secret Scroll," she muttered with amazement.

"You recognize it?" Catty asked.

Maggie nodded, still too stunned to say more. When she was finally able to speak, her voice seemed filled with awe. "I had always thought the existence of the Secret Scroll was only a legend. I never imagined it was real. Tradition maintains that the manuscript was hidden to protect the ultimate secret forever."

"What secret?" Serena asked.

Maggie hesitated. "The Path of the Manuscript," she breathed. "It reveals how to destroy the Atrox."

"How?" Vanessa asked and peered over

Maggie's shoulder as if she could read the spiraling script.

"That's amazing," Catty voiced the excitement for all of them.

"What do we do first?" Jimena asked eagerly.

"Have patience," Maggie warned. "You must not rush forward. Every act has good and evil consequences. I need time to read the manuscript and consider all its possibilities."

"Why was it given to me?" Catty wondered.

Maggie looked at her solemnly. "According to the legend, it would mean that you are the designated heir." Her voice sounded filled with sadness and Catty wondered what Maggie wasn't telling her. Maggie seemed to read her concern. "The heir is the one chosen to follow the Path of the Manuscript."

Catty felt new anxiety take hold. "But how can I follow the Path when I can't even read the manuscript?"

"Don't worry, Catty." Maggie touched her gently. "It wouldn't have been given to you if you weren't up to the task."

The words provided little comfort. Catty knew Maggie was holding back.

"Tell Maggie about the Followers you saw," Jimena reminded her.

Maggie looked up, her eyes questioning.

"They looked older than any Followers I've seen before and they were too perfect-looking," Catty said.

Maggie glanced at her oddly. "What do you mean *perfect-looking*?"

"They looked like they'd just spent an hour in makeup on some movie set. You know, like politicians going on TV for a debate. Every hair in perfect order. Clothes perfectly pressed. They also had this strange electrical aura."

Maggie raised a quizzical eyebrow.

"The room seemed to fill with an electrical charge when they came in," Catty explained. "Their presence even affected the lights."

Maggie nodded in understanding. "Don't be deceived by their appearance. They weren't Followers."

"But I'm positive they were," Catty answered.

"Me, too," Vanessa agreed.

Maggie held up her hand. "They weren't Followers. They were Regulators."

"Regulators," Serena repeated with a worried expression. She tried to hide her concern, but Catty knew it was there. Her relationship with Stanton was forbidden, and the Atrox punished Followers who violated the taboo by sending Regulators to terminate them. Stanton had been willing to risk everything for Serena until he realized he was also putting her in danger.

Maggie looked at Serena as if she knew what she was thinking. "Yes, but I am confident that these Regulators are here for the manuscript. The Atrox wants it destroyed."

"Are you sure?" Serena asked apprehensively.

"The Regulators Catty has described are the fiercest class," Maggie continued. "They are so committed to the Atrox, that their very appearance becomes distorted and twisted by its evil until they look monstrous."

"But they looked perfect." Catty seemed confused.

"Yes, dear." Maggie touched her arm gently. "They looked perfect because they can conceal their hideous appearance. Most choose to appear like distinguished adults because it is easier to gain trust that way. They can just as easily appear as a younger person. But altering their appearance takes tremendous energy and fortunately they are weaker when disguised."

"But what about when they're not disguised?" Jimena wondered.

Maggie sighed. "They are extremely powerful. Their greatest power is their ability to enter dreams."

"Dreams?" Vanessa asked uneasily and pulled at a strand of hair.

Maggie nodded. "These Regulators are free to travel about the dreamland. Every night they scan the dreamscape, searching. In fact, most people have seen them in their dreams but they think they've only had a nightmare."

Catty thought of the number of times she had awakened in the morning and found her lights still blazing because a nightmare had made her too afraid to sleep in the dark. Had the Regulators frightened her? Then she thought of Kendra's dream and another chill passed through her.

"The dream realm is an easy way for the Regulators to find a person who is trying to escape the Atrox," Maggie went on.

"How?" Serena asked uneasily.

"Once in a person's dream, they can scan a person's memories," Maggie explained. "Memories are like fingerprints, unique to the individual, and an infallible way to identify someone. These Regulators can also use dreams to enter a person's conscience and control them."

Maggie studied the manuscript again. "I'm confident that the sudden arrival of these Regulators is somehow associated with the manuscript, even though all Regulators are terrified by it."

"Why would they be afraid of it?" Vanessa asked.

"Because Regulators believe in the manuscript's curse, and yet their allegiance to the Atrox demands that they search for it and destroy it. I don't need to remind you to be alert and careful. The Atrox will do anything to destroy the manuscript. We'll meet after I've had a chance to study it."

"Shouldn't we follow the first step?" Jimena asked.

Maggie smiled. "I admire the way you are always ready to act. But let me spend some time with the manuscript first. After all, I had always believed it was only legend."

Maggie stuffed the manuscript into her canvas bag. She walked away from them and didn't look back.

Jimena sighed. "Let's go over to Westwood and get something to eat."

"I'll catch up with you." Catty suddenly remembered the moon amulet that had belonged to her mother. She ran after Maggie.

Maggie turned and placed a hand on Catty's shoulder.

"I forgot to show you this," Catty announced and pulled the amulet from her pocket. The metal was dull and blackened and didn't reflect the light.

Maggie gasped and tried to cover her reaction.

"Well?" Catty asked impatiently.

"I'm afraid the amulet belongs to a Daughter who turned to the Atrox," Maggie answered.

CHAPTER NINE

CATTY HURRIED AWAY, pushing into the crowd of protesters. She didn't want Maggie to see the tears building in her eyes.

Maggie called after her but she pretended not to hear. When she was sure Maggie wasn't following her, she stopped and glanced down at the amulet in her hand. Now more than ever she wanted to see her mother. She clenched the tarnished silver charm tightly. If she could find a way to go that far back in time, perhaps she could help her.

Catty made an effort to compose herself as

she hurried toward Westwood Village below the UCLA campus. Normally she loved looking at the spires, domes, and minarets on the old buildings but right now she was too busy searching for her friends. She found them sitting around a table at a sidewalk cafe.

Jimena was adjusting her ankle bracelets. She looked unhappy. Serena sipped a glass of water, frowning in concentration. Vanessa nervously bit her fingernails.

Catty sat down. "What's up? I thought everyone would be really excited about the Scroll. It's what we've been waiting for."

"Listen up." Jimena nodded toward Serena.

"I was able to go inside Maggie's mind," Serena said simply.

"You've never been able to read Maggie's thoughts," Catty argued.

"I know," Serena agreed. "I didn't even really mean to, but I guess she was so distracted by the Scroll that her guard was down."

"Tell her what you read," Jimena urged.

"Maggie thinks the manuscript is sending

her to her death," Serena spoke the words slowly.

"No way," Catty exclaimed. "Why would Maggie think she's being sent to her death if the manuscript is the key to destroying the Atrox?"

"She wouldn't," Jimena answered.

"Not unless Maggie has somehow deceived us," Vanessa added quietly.

They stared at her in silence.

"How do you figure that?" Jimena picked up a menu, then set it back on the table with a slap.

Vanessa sipped her water, then finally answered. "Maybe she's really part of the Atrox and has been conning us. If that were true, then if the Atrox is destroyed, she'd be destroyed."

"How could you even think that?" Serena said angrily.

"Think about it," Vanessa stated. "Maggie stops us from acting. I mean, our instincts tell us to do the dangerous thing, but she always cautions against it."

"Because she cares for us," Jimena reminded her.

"And besides," Serena put in. "If we do something that she's asked us not to do, she's never upset. In fact, she usually says that it was exactly what she wanted us to do anyway."

"So maybe she tells us not to do something," Catty suggested, "because she's really testing us to see if we have what it takes."

Vanessa shrugged. "It's a possibility."

"But you're thinking something else." Jimena sounded exasperated.

"Come on," Vanessa continued. "Catty was given the manuscript. She's the only person who can follow the Path, and yet Maggie takes it from her. Shouldn't it stay with Catty?"

"She took it because she's going to study it," Catty protested.

Vanessa started to say something more, but a deep voice interrupted. "Hey, how's my girl?"

They turned. Toby stood behind them. "I didn't know you guys liked to hang out in

Westwood. What are you talking about?"

"It's private," Serena snapped.

Toby smiled. "I could hear you guys arguing all the way inside, so it couldn't have been too private. What's this manuscript that you're talking about?"

"Nothing," Catty and Jimena said together.

Vanessa stood suddenly, and Toby's eyes admired her body. "You look great," he cooed and kissed her cheek.

"Let's go over to the campus." Vanessa took his arm. "I love to walk around there."

"Sure." He tried to pull her closer, but when he did, her hands went automatically to her chest in a protective way as if she were trying to make a barricade between them.

The gesture baffled Catty. Vanessa said she liked him, and yet her body language revealed the opposite.

"I'll call you tonight." Vanessa waved and left with Toby.

Catty watched Vanessa and Toby walk away

arm-in-arm down Westwood Boulevard. She reached for her water and accidentally touched Serena. A spark flew between them. "How'd that happen?"

"Dry, hot weather," Serena remarked blandly.

"I thought it was dry, cold weather," Catty offered.

"Does Toby creep you guys out as much as he does me?" Serena asked.

Catty nodded. "He's cute with that dark goatee and great bod, but his smile makes me uneasy. I don't know why Vanessa likes him so much."

"He's too clean cut," Jimena interrupted. "I like guys who are a little roughed up."

"You better," Serena joked. "Collin always has a peeling nose and sand in his ears."

Jimena laughed. "Yeah, but he's the best-looking guy I've ever met." Collin was Serena's surf rat brother and Jimena's boyfriend. "I'm counting the days until he gets back from Hawaii."

Catty glanced down at her watch. "Could

you give me a ride over to the bookshop? I can't be late again."

Twenty minutes later, Catty pushed through the front door of the Darma Bookstore on Third Street. Brass bells on leather cords tingled in harmony as she closed the door behind her. Books, candles, prayer beads, crystals, and essence oils sat on white shelves in neat arrays.

"Hi, Mom," Catty called. Incense curled sinuously around her and filled the air with a pungent scent.

Kendra glanced at her watch and a smile crossed her face. "Thanks for being on time." She picked up a stack of papers and started for the back door. "What should I pick up for dinner?"

"Anything," Catty answered.

"That's dangerous." Kendra gave her a teasing grin.

"No health food," Catty added. "Something with lots of fat and calories."

"Order pizza, then," Kendra called over her shoulder.

"Sounds good," Catty answered.

After Kendra left, Catty wandered around the bookstore. It always made her feel tranquil. Water bubbled from fountains set in stone planters near the door, and soothing guitar music played from the speakers.

Catty pushed through the blue curtains separating the back room from the store and went into the small kitchen. She sat down at the oak table. A blurred photo of a flying saucer hovering over the Arizona desert hung on the wall next to posters of deep space taken from the Hubble telescope. Kendra thought the pictures would comfort Catty.

Catty pulled out her mother's moon amulet and set it on the table in front of her. She wondered if Maggie was right. Could her mother have turned to the Atrox? Or was there some other reason the amulet was with her mother's belongings? She wished she could go into the past and see her mother right now. Then she remembered what Serena had said about Maggie. Before she could consider it more, the bells hanging on the front door tingled. She put the amulet back in her pocket and walked into the shop.

Chris stood near a counter, looking at a pack of green candles.

"Hi," he called when he saw her.

"I didn't know you were coming by." She felt happy to see him, but she couldn't spend time with him right now. She had too many things she needed to sort out. Plus it was against Kendra's new rules to have guys visit while Catty watched the shop, and she didn't want to chance getting in trouble again.

"I missed you after school," he said with a flirtatious smile. "You didn't stick around."

She was surprised that he had noticed, but she was glad that he had. She shrugged. "I had to go someplace."

"Anywhere special?"

She cocked her head and looked at him. If she hadn't known better, she'd think he was jealous. "Just out," she answered lightly.

"Not with someone else, I hope." He tried to

make it sound like he was teasing, but she sensed his worry.

"Not with another guy, if that's what you mean." She looked at him curiously.

He took her hand. "Is that what you think I mean?"

"Look, I really am busy." She wanted him to leave. What if Kendra suddenly came back? "I have a lot of things I need to do."

He acted like he hadn't heard her. He stepped closer and with the tip of his finger, he turned her face up to his. His breath was sweet and tickled across her cheek. He rested his hands on her shoulders, then slid them down her arms to her elbows. He pulled her to him and placed her hands behind his back.

He draped his arms around her. "I really am sorry about the way I acted at school. Can you just trust me for now?"

"Can't you tell me what's going on?" She glanced at his sensuous lips.

He shook his head. "I want to tell you. I will someday. I promise."

She looked into his alluring eyes. She wanted to believe him. More than anything, and if she were only going by the way her heart felt, she would trust him.

"I really like you." He spoke softly and the words floated around her in a dreamy way. "More than I've ever liked anyone and if you knew everything about me, you'd know that means a lot."

She started to ask him to explain, but before she could he bent down. She thought he was going to kiss her, but he let his lips tease, hovering inches from hers. Their breath mingled. When his lips finally touched hers, a pleasant shock went through her.

All the worries that had been building inside her seemed to vanish and there was only Chris and the sensations of her body. She had imagined so often what it must feel like to kiss a guy, but even in her wildest fantasies a kiss had never felt as good as the ones Chris gave her.

When he pulled back, she opened her eyes quickly and caught a look of intense longing in his eyes, and then it was gone. Was it only her imagination?

"Chris . . ." She started to ask him what was bothering him, but he closed her mouth with another kiss.

CHAPTER TEN

CATTY SAT IN geometry class nervously waiting for Mr. Hall to hand back the test papers. He stepped down the aisle and paused in front of her desk, tapping his toe. He gazed suspiciously at her through the lens of his small black-framed glasses, then set a paper on her desk.

A large red *A* looped across of the top. She tried to pick up the paper but her hands trembled so badly that kids sitting on either side of her were starting to stare. She had been the first one to finish the test the day before, not because she had studied, but because the test questions were a duplicate of the ones on the test found in her mother's belongings.

She stared at the paper and took a deep breath. She wanted to compare the new and old tests, but she knew if she pulled out the old one, Mr. Hall would see and accuse her of cheating.

Finally, she couldn't take the wondering any longer. She grabbed her bag and the new test paper and went up to Mr. Hall's desk.

"Can I have the hall pass?" she whispered.

He scowled and wiped his handkerchief across his nose. "Class just began."

"Girl stuff," she confided in an even lower whisper.

Mr. Hall dug the large wood board from his desk and handed it to her. "Don't lose it this time, Catty."

"I promise I won't." She grinned nervously. How could she ever explain that she had lost the last hall pass somewhere in time?

She hurried from the room. Jimena, Serena, and Vanessa all cast worried looks after her.

In the corridor, she walked quickly past open

doors. Teachers' voices drifted into the hallway after her. She went outside to the back of the school and found a cement bench near the weed-infested corridor between the gym and music building. The rays from the morning sun dusted the side of the stucco wall but did little to warm her. She sat down and spread the first paper in front of her, then searched for the old one in her bag, found it, and smoothed it next to the new one. She let out a long hiss. They were identical. Even the red As were a perfect match.

She stared at the papers for a long time, wondering what it meant. She was about to go back to class when a shadow slid over the papers.

Even as she was turning to see who it was, she could feel her moon amulet pulsing against her chest. Her body became vigilant and tense.

Stanton stood behind her, dressed in black, his shaggy blond hair hanging in his eyes. He was handsome in a dangerous way that made her want to stare forever in his intense blue eyes.

"Catty." His voice sounded annoyed.

"What?" she answered coldly. She grabbed her bag and took a step backward.

Catty often wondered what evil act Stanton had committed to receive the gift of immortality from the Atrox. It didn't matter that Serena liked him. Catty saw him as purely evil. Besides, she never believed that Stanton really cared about Serena. She assumed he was only using her. There was immense competition among Followers for a place of power in the Atrox hierarchy and the biggest prize for any Followers was the seduction of a Daughter of the Moon or the theft of her powers.

She stuffed the two test papers back in her bag and stood to face him. Before she was even aware that his hand had moved, he ripped the bag from her.

"Give it back." She started to reach for it but already he had opened it and was digging inside.

When he didn't find what he wanted, he tossed the bag back to her. "I've been told you possess the Secret Scroll." His voice rumbled with anger. "Where is it?"

Catty felt her body preparing to fight. She

stood taller, anticipating his attack. "Like I'm going to give you that."

"The manuscript belongs to my family," Stanton spoke calmly. She tried not to look in his eyes but it was hard not to stare at their haunting beauty.

"What makes you think it belonged to your family?" she challenged. "I'm the heir."

A darkness seemed to pass over his face. "There was a quest for the Secret Scroll at the end of the thirteenth century. My father found it. It belongs to me now."

Without warning, his mind was in hers before she could deflect it. Her heart beat nervously, but it didn't feel as if he meant to harm her. He seemed to be holding back as if he didn't want to frighten her. Abruptly his memories came in a fast-moving torrent, spinning and swirling around her in an ever increasing speed until she had to reach out and clutch his arm to keep from falling. Finally, the dizzy motion stopped and she focused on one memory.

It opened before her, and Catty hesitatingly

stepped forward. Stanton had once trapped Vanessa in one of his memories but while there she had tried to save a younger Stanton from the Atrox. For that act he could never harm Vanessa, but Catty had no guarantee. Stanton was capable of trapping her forever in his memories. Still, she felt awed by what was happening, but she didn't feel afraid.

She stepped onto a hard floor and almost tripped on an animal skin. Crosses and candles were placed around the small room. Tapestries hung on the stone walls and a fire crackled in a corner. Three men sat around a table that was covered with a delicately woven cloth. Two of the men wore the cowled robe of monks. Catty couldn't see their faces. Then she saw what held their attention. The Secret Scroll lay in the middle of the table.

The third man glanced at the fire. He resembled Stanton. Vanessa had told her that Stanton's father had been a great prince of western Europe during the thirteenth century. He had raised an army to go on a crusade against the Atrox, but then the Atrox had kidnapped Stanton to stop his father.

At first, she couldn't understand their language, but Stanton must have done something, because suddenly she grasped what they were saying.

"My mission has always been to combat evil by force of arms." Stanton's father spoke quietly. "Not by prayers." His voice was gentle and kind, and it stirred something inside of Catty.

"The Path of the Manuscript is the only way," said one of the monks.

Stanton's father nodded. "I've already chosen my path." He walked to the fireplace and stared at the flames. "But the manuscript must be guarded until an heir is found. Someone of pure heart who can fight the Atrox if I fail." He turned back suddenly and faced the monks again. "And even if the Atrox takes me, you are not to exchange the manuscript for my freedom."

The monks nodded again.

Stanton's father continued, "I have two sons.

One surely will survive and when he is of age you will give the manuscript to him."

The monks turned toward the corner of the room. Seated on a tall chair sat a small boy with blond hair. She knew he must be Stanton at a younger age. Even then his blue eyes were alluring. He looked frightened by what was going on around him.

"We've already named a keeper for the manuscript," one monk asserted. "A knight who is strong and noble, and will risk his life to guard it."

Stanton's father sat back at the table. "That is all, then."

The monks wrapped the parchment in a leather pouch and slowly left the room.

The memory began to fade, but Catty didn't want to leave this man. She wanted to talk to him. The edges of her vision shimmered, and then she was back in La Brea High facing Stanton.

"Now you see that it is mine," he said bluntly. "And I expect its return."

Catty shook her head and took one step away from him. "I was given the manuscript—"

"Its curse brings horrible danger to its owner," he warned. "Are you prepared for that?"

She hadn't really thought about the curse. Both Maggie and Kendra had mentioned it, but it had seemed more superstition than reality until now.

"It's not real?" She had meant for the words to form a statement but instead it sounded like a question.

"Throughout its history the manuscript has cursed its possessor."

Catty hesitated. Was that why Maggie had seemed so frightened by the manuscript?

"The Daughters of the Moon should stay as far away from the Secret Scroll as possible," Stanton cautioned.

Catty considered his warning, but she didn't trust Stanton, so how could she believe anything he told her? "You only want the manuscript so you can turn it over to the Atrox and win a place of honor in the Inner Circle."

"Inner Circle," Stanton repeated with obvious

disdain. "How little you know." His mouth opened as if he were going to say more, but then he turned his head, seeming to sense something.

He reached for Catty and she took a quick step away from him.

"Come with me," he ordered and held out his hand.

"I'm not going anywhere with you," Catty answered.

"I warned you," he said, and then he slipped around the music building and peeked back at her. "Hurry. Can't you feel it?"

She clutched her bag against her chest. There was an unusual stillness in the air. "What's happening?"

"The Regulators." He motioned for her to join him. "Come on, we have to escape into time."

She shook her head. "Why should I take you back in time and save you? I don't care if Regulators terminate you. It's just one less Follower I have to worry about."

"You understand nothing." The scorn in his voice made her hesitate. "There's still time," he continued. "Take us back to the day you were abandoned on the side of the road."

Catty felt a chill pass through her. "How do you know I was abandoned?" Then she remembered Serena and felt suddenly irritated. How many secrets had Serena shared with him?

Footsteps pounded on the cement behind her. She turned. The three Regulators from the coroner's office walked toward her. She glanced the other way and saw Stanton disappear down the corridor.

"Wait for me," she whispered and started running. When she was at the end of the corridor, she looked for Stanton.

He grabbed her hand and pulled her into the boy's restroom, then into one of the stalls. She was pushed up against him.

"Take us back," he ordered.

"You don't understand," Catty confessed. "I've never been able to time-travel that far back without getting stuck."

Footsteps sounded near the bathroom door.

"Take my hand," Stanton ordered.

"Why?" she asked.

"We have no time left." He held out his hand. "Do you want to escape?"

She stared at Stanton. Could she trust him?

CHAPTER ELEVEN

CATTY TOOK STANTON'S hand and his tremendous power surged through her. The bathroom stall wavered, then broke apart before exploding into a flash of white light. Stanton's hand clasped hers tightly, and they were sucked into the tunnel. His speed was much greater than hers. The free fall made her stomach ripple and she had difficulty breathing. She now knew why Vanessa hated time travel. Catty couldn't pull air into her lungs and at the moment when she thought she might pass out, they fell from the tunnel back into time.

Stanton landed on his feet, but Catty skid-ded across scorched dusty ground. She lay in the hot sand, gasping for air. Stanton paced, his shadow brushing back and forth over her. The blazing sun stung her arms and face.

Suddenly she sat up with a jerk. Tall spiny cacti surrounded her.

She stood abruptly in spite of her dizziness and wiped the sand and dirt from her face. She took an awkward step backward and surveyed the vast landscape. Wisps of black smoke came from a nearby arroyo. She ran to the edge of the craggy embankment and peered over. The air was filled with the stench of burning rubber and oil.

The charred skeleton of a crashed car sat on the rocky bottom. The sight jogged a memory. She remembered the crash and the fire. Only now she realized she hadn't been inside the car, but outside watching from the ledge as she was now.

Stanton gently touched her arm and pointed. Her heart caught. There she was at age six, wandering down the highway in her sandals, baggy red shorts, and a large floppy hat that kept trying to blow off her head.

Tears burned into her eyes. Stanton put his hand on her shoulder as the tears fell down her cheeks.

"Stanton," a voice called with sudden urgency.

Catty sucked in her breath. "My mother?"

"Yes," he said.

Her heart beat crazily. She turned slowly.

A slender woman with large brown eyes and thick sun-kissed hair walked toward them. She wore cutoff jeans and a man's white T-shirt. Her knees and hands were scraped and bleeding.

"Stanton," her mother repeated.

"She knows you?" Catty glanced at Stanton. How could her mother know him?

"Please, Stanton." Her mother pointed to the smaller Catty walking in the distance. "Take my daughter's memories from her so she'll be safe."

"I can't, Zoe," he whispered.

Catty glanced from Stanton to her mother.

He even knew her name. How was that possible?

"Please," Zoe pleaded again. "If she has no memories, the Regulators won't be able to find her. You must save her."

In spite of the heat, Catty began trembling. Why had Regulators been after her when she was only a child?

Stanton stared off at the younger Catty walking down the roadway.

"Do you want what happened to you, to happen to her?" Zoe spoke in a low tone. "She's only a child like you were."

Stanton hesitated, then took three steps forward. Catty watched his eyes focus and narrow.

"Thank you." Zoe sighed with relief and closed her eyes.

"It's done." Stanton turned back and Zoe seemed to relax then.

"Maybe now she'll even be able to live a normal life." Zoe wiped at her eyes.

Catty heard the whisper of tires on the hot

pavement and turned. Kendra's old Impala pulled to the side of the road. She couldn't hear what Kendra was saying to the younger Catty, but she knew she was asking Catty if she was okay.

Catty watched Zoe's reaction. "Be good to her," Zoe whispered, and then she fell against Stanton.

Little Catty climbed into the car with Kendra.

"Why aren't they leaving?" Zoe asked nervously.

"Be patient, Zoe," Stanton murmured.

Catty climbed over several boulders and perched on the top of a small hill so she could watch both her mother and Kendra's car.

The sun was at a lower angle and the saguaro cacti cast long shadows across the desert floor when Kendra's car finally pulled away. Catty climbed down from her perch on the hill. Her face prickled with the feel of sunburn.

"She's safe now." Zoe blinked away the tears forming in the corner of her eyes. She turned to

Stanton with a smile that did little to conceal her sadness. Then she seemed to notice Catty for the first time.

"Who's your friend?" Zoe asked Stanton. She glanced at Catty's moon amulet and then her eyes bore into Catty's.

"Zoe," Stanton said. "I want you to meet your daughter."

Zoe glanced at Stanton in disbelief, then stared at Catty in openmouthed wonder. Her hand reached out and caressed Catty's cheek, touched her lips, and smoothed back her hair. "I see your father in your face," she uttered more to herself than to Catty. Then a slight smile crossed her lips. "I give you away and you return to me the same day. At least I know you do make it safely into the future." She started to embrace Catty.

Catty closed her eyes waiting for her mother's hug. She had imagined this so many times—but Zoe pulled back suddenly.

"This is too dangerous," she declared, and new anxiety filled her eyes. "You must leave. The

Regulators are always watching me."

Then she turned to Stanton. "Why did you bring her here?"

Catty glanced at Stanton and wondered if it had been a trap after all.

"I wanted you to tell her about the Secret Scroll," Stanton replied smoothly.

"She's received it already?" Zoe asked and seemed surprised; then her shoulders slumped in anguish, and she raked her fingers through her hair. "How can that be?"

Catty wondered why her mother was so distressed.

Zoe's eyes nervously studied the horizon. "You must take her back before the Regulators come."

"But . . ." Catty began. "Why have Regulators always been after me? I thought Regulators only terminated Followers who rebelled against the Atrox, or didn't follow the Atrox's orders? What would they want with me?"

Zoe scanned the desert, then turned back to

Catty. "There's no time for me to explain now. Give me your address and I'll find you in the future. That's the best I can do."

Catty fumbled in her bag for a piece of paper, found one, pulled it out, and scribbled her name and address across the top. She handed the paper to her mother.

"I'll find you, later, when it's safe. I promise." She hugged Catty, then gently pushed her back to Stanton. "Take her now."

Catty looked at the paper in her mother's hands and with a shock realized she had written her name and address on today's geometry test paper.

Stanton grabbed her wrist and the air shimmered.

"Wait," Catty yelled. She reached into her bag and pulled out the blackened moon amulet and gave it to her mother. "Here."

"You have it?" Her mother seemed shocked. "I thought it had been taken from me." She held it tenderly and fastened it around her neck.

Catty smiled at her. "See you in the future."

Her mother looked up and smiled back. "See you."

Stanton reached for Catty's hand and his energy rushed through her.

Her mother looked desperate. "Don't trust Maggie," Zoe yelled after them and then she mouthed, "I love you," as her face contorted with sadness.

The desert landscape wiggled, then broke apart as if it were a sheet of glass. They were whisked into the tunnel as an explosion of brilliant light filled the air. Catty squinted her eyes, emotions roiling through her. She thought about her mother and then about Maggie. Why would her mother tell her not to trust Maggie?

They landed on a quiet street near Catty's house. It was already dark and the only sound was that of sprinklers watering a nearby lawn. Stanton caught her before she fell to the ground.

"So now you know that the Scroll has put you in grave danger," Stanton stated.

Catty nodded.

"If you'll give it to me," he offered, "you'll be safe."

Catty couldn't bring herself to trust him. "Why aren't you afraid of the curse?"

He smiled bitterly. "Because I am already cursed."

The words chilled her. She almost felt sorry for him.

"My offer stands," he whispered and then he dissolved into shadow.

She stood in the darkness and wondered why he so desperately wanted the manuscript if not to give it to the Atrox. Still he didn't seem as bad as she had once thought. She could almost understand why Serena liked him so much.

Catty wondered what it was that made her mother trust Stanton. She held the memory of her mother's face in her mind and started walking home.

A few minutes later, Catty brushed against the pink oleanders that grew in front of their redwood fence. She crossed the porch as a gentle breeze stirred and the wind chimes tingled.

She opened the door, went inside, and locked the door behind her. She had expected Kendra to be waiting for her, having fits because she hadn't gotten home in time to watch the store, but the house was as silent as a tomb and dark, except for the light coming through the windows from the street lamps.

For just a fleeting second she felt as if Stanton hadn't transported them far enough into the future and that she could run up the stairs as she had when she was younger and find Kendra in bed, reading. Then Kendra would run her bathwater and she could fall into her own bed without a worry. She wished things were still that easy.

She sighed and walked into the kitchen. She switched on the overhead lights. The clock read nine o'clock.

She reached for the telephone to call Vanessa. Her mother answered.

"Is Vanessa there?" Catty spoke into the receiver.

"Hi, Catty," Vanessa's mother greeted her.

"Vanessa's at the party with Toby. Aren't you going?"

Catty had forgotten the party.

The doorbell rang. She knew that it would be Chris.

CHAPTER TWELVE

CATTY OPENED THE door. Chris smiled at her. He smelled of spicy aftershave and looked cuter than ever.

"I've been trying to call you all afternoon." He walked into the house and handed her a bouquet of red roses.

"Thanks." As they walked into the kitchen, she breathed in the scent of the roses.

In the brighter light he glanced at her, then took a longer look, lingering on her clothes and feet. An odd expression crossed his face. She suddenly became aware that she was covered with desert dust, sunburned, and sweating. She could only imagine what she must look like. She touched her cheek and wondered if it was still covered with sand.

"I've been working in the yard," she lied and took a vase from under the sink.

"At nine o'clock at night?" he asked with a wry smile.

She ran water into the vase. "Chris, I really can't go to the party with you tonight."

He leaned over the breakfast bar and smiled at her. This time she noticed his clean, even teeth, so white and healthy as if he had been eating apples all his life. She wanted to kiss him but instead she turned away.

"Why not?" he asked. "All you need to do is take a quick shower. You don't have to dress up. No one is."

She slipped the flowers into the water and set the vase on the counter. "I feel too tired. And I just need time to think. Don't you ever want to be alone sometimes?"

"Sure." He stepped around the counter and stopped close to her. She glanced up and saw herself reflected in his pupils. His fingers played on her shoulders.

"I'd like to be alone with you," he whispered slowly. "We could stay here and watch videos." His hands smoothed down her arms and then he held both of her hands. He didn't seem to mind that they were dirty.

"That's not what I had in mind," she answered.

"But I don't want you to miss the party." His words rustled across her right ear. He took one more step and this time he was close enough to kiss her. His thigh rubbed against hers. She shivered with pleasure.

"Please come." The word fell on her ears like a caress and he looked at her in a dreamy sort of way that made her feel giddy. "Come to the party with me, Catty."

He leaned over and traced one finger gently over her chin and down her throat. She leaned back and let him kiss her.

"Come to the party," he said between his kisses.

She hated to think that she was the kind of girl who would do things just because she liked the way a guy kissed her.

Finally, she pulled away from him. "I'll take a quick shower."

"Great." He grinned.

They drove over to the hills in Brentwood. The smoky smell from the fires was stronger here, and Catty's eyes burned. Finally, at the top of the hill, Chris pulled his battered Volvo to the curb and got out. Catty heard the music as she stepped from the car. Chris took her hand and they walked up to a huge house with massive columns and an ornate iron fence.

"Whose house is it?" she asked as they walked through the front room.

"Jerome's," Chris answered. "The guy who plays drums in the marching band. His uncle's an entertainment lawyer."

She followed Chris through French doors that led to a large patio. It was already crowded with kids dancing. On the other side of the pool, a band played on a cement terrace. A heavy metal band hammered out notes with complete reck-lessness. Kids in black pressed against the plat-form, head-banging in time to the hard rock music.

"The music will change soon," Chris spoke into her ear. "Then we can dance."

She leaned against Chris. She liked the feel of his arm around her waist. Now she was glad she had come to the party.

She started to say *Let's go look at the view*, when Chris suddenly withdrew his arm.

"What's wrong?" she asked.

He shook his head but he didn't look at her. His eyes searched through the crowd of dancers, jostling around them. She followed his look and wondered if he had recognized someone.

"Listen." He took a quick step away from her. "Would you like something to eat?"

She shook her head. "I'm fine."

But he was already stepping away from her. "I'll just get us a couple of Cokes." He turned and left her without looking back.

She sighed and sat down on a patio chair that had been moved out to the grass under the jacaranda trees. Chris ran around the pool and across the lawn to a metal table that was piled high with soft drinks and ice. He took two Cokes, but instead of coming back to her, he went inside the house.

She wondered briefly what he was doing. She sat back and waited impatiently. By the time Chris returned, the heavy metal band had finished playing and three guys from La Brea High took the terrace and started rapping. Their footwork was fast. Their right arms punched down as their left legs kicked back.

"Here."

She turned back. Chris handed her a Coke, then sat on the lawn next to her chair. He opened a napkin filled with cookies.

"Try a cookie," he offered and bit into an oatmeal raisin.

She hesitated a moment, then spoke clearly, "Chris, maybe you should just take me home."

"Home?" He looked wounded.

"Well, you're not acting like you want to be with me or you wouldn't have run off as soon as we got here."

"I thought you'd want something to eat," he protested.

"I told you I didn't."

"I want to spend the evening with you," he explained. "Why else would I have asked you? I thought we could have a good time." But even as he spoke, his eyes started scanning the kids standing around the terrace.

"Look," Catty continued. "I don't want to share you with anyone else."

His eyes shot back to her.

"You're always looking around like you're afraid someone is going to see us together. That means only one thing to me."

"What?" He looked confused.

"That you have another girlfriend."

He looked at her in disbelief. "Thanks," he whispered.

"Thanks?" she repeated. Now it was her turn to feel surprised. "What do you mean, *thanks*?"

"Thanks because it means you think we shouldn't see other people." He looked happy.

"I didn't say that," she protested.

"But it implies you want us to be exclusive."

"I said I didn't want to share you." She thought a moment, then smiled. "Okay, it means exclusive, but something has been bothering you. You've been acting so—"

He jumped up. "I'll be right back," he interrupted. "I forgot to get pizza." He ran toward the house.

Catty cursed. It had been a big mistake to come to the party. She should have stayed home as she had originally planned. She looked up.

Jimena and Serena walked through the back gate on the other side of the pool. They were dressed in leather like biker chicks. Serena had on platform boots, a tight-fitting motorcycle jacket, and a mini. Jimena wore studded ankle boots, a bareback leather halter top, and a hip-hugging matching skirt.

Catty pushed through the crowd of kids dancing near the edge of the pool and joined them.

"Where'd you get the clothes?" she asked.

"Vanessa's mom," Serena answered. "You should have come."

Vanessa's mother worked as a costume designer for the movies. She wore clothes before anyone even knew they were in style. That was her job. She had to be a year or two ahead of everyone else. Sometimes it embarrassed Vanessa to have a mother so overly trendy. But Catty loved to go over to their house and try on her mother's designs.

"I wish I could have." Catty admired the slinky outfits. "But I went back in time. I need to talk to all of you about it. It's really important. Where's Vanessa?"

"Check it out." Jimena motioned to the patio where kids were dancing.

In the middle of the bobbing bodies, Vanessa moved sinuously against Toby. She wore a black leather skirt with a long slit up the side and a cropped leather jacket. Her midriff was bare and looked incredibly good with the gold chains that hung around her waist.

"Vanessa," Catty gasped.

Serena stared at Vanessa. "What do you think?"

"Since when does she dress like that?" Catty asked. Vanessa always dressed stylishly, but conservatively. "This is very un-Vanessa."

"Toby picked it out for her," Jimena put in.

Vanessa rolled her head and looked up at Toby. Maybe she did like him, Catty thought.

Toby's fingers kept running over her bare waist, and whenever he pulled her close to him his lips moved to her cheek as if they were sharing secrets. Still, Catty couldn't erase the feeling that something was wrong. Vanessa kept looking away.

Catty glanced around the room and found Michael. He was watching Vanessa and he wasn't even bothering to hide his jealousy. Other girls were coming up to him and flirting with him, but his eyes kept going back to her.

The music stopped, and Vanessa ran over to them.

"So where were you?" Vanessa asked. "You missed all the fun."

"I went back to see my mother," Catty announced.

The girls stared at her in disbelief.

Jimena was the first to speak. "Let's go back by the refreshment table," Jimena suggested. "So we can talk in private."

"How did you go back that far?" Serena asked as they walked past a row of azalea bushes.

"Stanton took me," Catty replied.

"Stanton?" Serena's eyes widened. "You saw him? Is he okay?"

Catty nodded. "He's fine. He helped me escape the Regulators and then get back to see my mother."

Serena smiled sadly. "I'm glad he's okay." But her expression told Catty that she also still missed him.

When they were next to the metal table, Jimena picked up a Pepsi and snapped the top, then turned to Catty. "So what happened?"

Catty told them everything about the afternoon. Serena kept interrupting to ask more questions about Stanton, but finally Catty finished. Then she hesitated and added, "I think it was a mistake to give the manuscript to Maggie."

"Why?" Vanessa looked surprised and worried.

Catty spoke carefully. "Just as I was leaving my mother told me not to trust Maggie."

"Maybe you didn't hear her correctly," Serena offered.

Catty shook her head. "I know that's what she said."

Jimena pondered. "But I trust Maggie."

"Me, too," Catty said. "But I'm worried. I want to get the manuscript back from her."

Jimena shook her head. "It's better if we leave it with Maggie."

"Why?" Catty asked.

"Because," Jimena said slowly. "I had a premonition."

"What did you see?" Vanessa asked.

Jimena stared at Catty. "I saw Catty destroy the manuscript."

Catty gasped. "Me? Are you sure? But I'm the heir."

Jimena nodded gravely.

"Your premonitions aren't always how they appear," Serena suggested. "So maybe it's not as bad as it seems."

Catty looked at Jimena. She believed Jimena, but she had a strange feeling of intuition of her own. She felt something treacherous in the air and somehow it was associated with the manuscript and Maggie.

"But." Vanessa was thinking as she spoke. "If the manuscript is evil it needs to be destroyed."

"What do you mean evil?" Serena asked. "If it's supposed to help us destroy the Atrox, it can't be evil."

"But we don't know if that's true yet," Vanessa argued. "We don't really know anything about the manuscript or the guy who gave it to Catty."

"He didn't seem evil," Catty explained, thinking of the mysterious guy. "He seemed . . ." She searched for a word. "Magnanimous."

"What if the Path is actually a fraud?" Vanessa pointed out. "Maybe it's a trick from the Atrox."

"What's the Atrox?" a voice said.

They stopped talking and turned. Toby stood behind them, smiling and sipping on a Coke. Had he been listening to their entire conversation?

Catty glared at Vanessa and pulled her to the other side of the table. Serena and Jimena followed. Toby leaned against the fence and watched them. "Why is your boyfriend always eavesdropping on our conversations?" Catty demanded.

"He's not." Vanessa seemed indignant. "He's just trying to be friendly."

"You were complaining about Michael not giving you space," Catty accused. "Toby doesn't even let you breathe."

"Well, if you like Michael so much," Vanessa answered coldly, "then you date him."

"Catty's not the only person who's getting bugged by the way Toby is always around," Serena added.

"Look," Vanessa explained. "Just give him a chance. I feel really connected to him."

Serena and Jimena exchanged surprised looks.

"Vanessa." Catty hesitated before continuing. "To everyone else, it seems like you still like Michael. You're always looking to see where he is—"

Vanessa shook her head. "I like Toby. I can't get him out of my mind."

"Hey, are you talking about me?" Toby was beside them again. How had he crept up so quietly?

The new band began to play a swing tune.

Toby took Vanessa's hand. "Let's go show them what we learned in class."

"Okay," Vanessa squealed. "Come on. You guys gotta come back to the patio so you can see what I can do now."

As they started back, Catty's hand brushed against the table. A spark connected between her fingers and the metal edge of the table. Her hand shot back in surprise. "Weird," she muttered to herself.

"Look at Vanessa." Jimena pointed.

Toby and Vanessa started dancing the Lindy. Vanessa turned beneath Toby's raised arm, then he pulled her close against his body before he swung her out again. They kicked sideways. Toby grabbed Vanessa, hooked her over his arm, and she seemed to fly over his back.

Kids applauded.

"Can you believe it?" Serena asked.

"She looks good," Catty agreed.

"Not her dancing," Serena explained. "I'm talking about the retro underwear she's wearing. Garters and all. So extremely cool."

Jimena laughed. "I guess love has really changed her."

"The only person Vanessa is fooling is herself," Catty said.

CHAPTER THiRTEEN

CATTY BACKED AWAY from the crowd and edged to the side of the house. The noise and music pounded through her head. Maybe it was the heat or the smoky smell from the lingering fires, because she didn't feel well. She wanted to go home, but she didn't see Chris anywhere and she didn't feel like walking or trying to catch a bus.

She strolled over wide stone steps, slipped past a hedge of oleanders and found a small rose garden that looked out over the city. Streetlights made a geometric pattern across the land below.

She sat on a small wrought-iron bench, breathed in deeply, and glanced at the moon.

She rubbed her forehead against the pain starting to spread through her head and tried to put everything that had happened that day in order. She was just starting to relax when a rustle of grass behind her made her start.

When the stealthy sound repeated, her head whipped around but a gloved hand stopped her.

"Don't look back." It was the voice of the mysterious man from the coroner's office.

Her heart raced. She hadn't known how badly she had wanted him to visit her again until she heard his voice. She wondered if she could actually be falling for a guy she didn't really know.

"Why haven't you acted?" His voice sounded angry and she caught something familiar in it. She concentrated, trying to identify it. "You're supposed to follow the Path of the manuscript."

"I gave the manuscript to someone," she explained.

"What?" Again she detected something in the voice that she had heard before, but where?

"I gave the manuscript to someone who guides me—" She tried to justify herself.

"You were never supposed to give it away. Don't you understand how dangerous that is?" Then his voice softened. "No, it's my fault. I should have explained more to you."

"What should you have explained?"

"I gave the manuscript to you because you are the heir, not someone else." His voice soothed her and she wondered if she was ever going to see his face. Then he continued, "The Secret Scroll can be dangerous in another person's hands."

"I'll get it back," Catty said with determination. "I promise."

"Good." He paused and she felt he wanted to say something more. She waited with rising anticipation but then his footsteps whispered through the grass behind her.

She knew he was leaving and she turned quickly, but he was gone.

"There you are." Chris brushed the oleanders aside, stumbled through the rosebushes, and sat on the bench next to her.

In the darkness she couldn't see the expression on his face clearly, but she hoped he couldn't see the irritation on hers.

She sighed and looked back at the moon, thinking about the mystery guy. Everything about him appealed to her. She was sure she could talk to him about all the things that had happened to her today. It was hard not being able to share those things with Chris.

"A penny for your thoughts." Chris rested his arm around her waist.

"Nothing." She shrugged.

"Tell me," he whispered.

She slowly shook her head.

"The way you're looking at the moon I'd say you have something really important on your mind."

"Maybe," she replied. "Can you take me home?"

She sensed his disappointment, but she didn't see any reason to stay. He'd just keep making excuses to leave her alone. Besides, she wanted to be home so she could think through her problems.

"Okay," he answered softly.

Chris walked her back through the party. As they started into the house, Jimena and Serena ran up to them and pulled her away from Chris.

"What did you decide?" Jimena asked.

"I'm going to leave the manuscript with Maggie," Catty lied. "You're right. It's safer if we let her keep it."

She hoped they couldn't read the lie in her words.

CHAPTER FOURTEEN

T he next morning, Catty awoke to the ringing telephone. She let the answering machine pick up. It was Vanessa, and her voice sounded anxious. Catty debated picking up the receiver, then decided against it. She had her own plans for the day. Maybe it was better if she didn't speak to Vanessa yet. Besides, she thought Vanessa probably only wanted to talk about Toby.

Chris called twice while she dressed in jeans and a comfy sweater. She didn't wait to hear his messages but left the house and walked down to the bus stop.

She rode the bus over to Cedars-Sinai Hospital, got off, and walked west on Alden Street until she came to Maggie's apartment. She nervously buzzed the security panel and wondered what she would say if Maggie answered. When Maggie's voice didn't come over the intercom, she knew she was in luck.

She randomly pressed five buzzers. Two voices answered.

"I locked myself out again," she lied and hoped no one inside would bother to come down to the entrance and see who it was.

Before she had even finished the sentence a loud hum opened the magnetic lock.

"Thanks," she yelled over her shoulder. She opened the door, hurried inside, and crossed the mirrored lobby. She kept her face down away from the security cameras although she doubted Maggie would ever report her crime to authorities. She stepped onto the elevator and pressed a button. The metal doors closed and the elevator carried her up to the fourth floor. The door opened with a loud grate that set her on edge.

Her heart pounded as she got off the elevator and walked down the narrow balcony that hung over a courtyard four stories below. A hummingbird hovered over the ivy growing around the iron railing.

She glanced behind her, then quickly removed the screen from the front window and set it aside. She pressed her hands flat against the glass and pushed upward and over. It worked. She'd learned that trick in sixth grade when she had been locked out of her own house.

Catty lifted one leg over the sill, then climbed in, closing and locking the window behind her. She walked quickly through the apartment and then back to the front door. After looking both ways, she hurried outside to the window and replaced the screen before going back into Maggie's apartment. She closed the door and rested against it, trying to will her heart to slow its beat.

The apartment loomed before her. It seemed so ordinary without its magical inhabitant. The walls were a grayish white and the lace panels hung lifeless over the sliding glass door that led to a private balcony. Maggie had no electrical appliances so there was no hum of a refrigerator or air conditioner.

She stepped down the narrow hallway and started exploring. She turned into the living room and a reflection in the mirror over the fireplace startled her. What she saw worried her. Her moon amulet was glowing. Why would it be glowing in Maggie's apartment? Was it trying to warn her of some danger? She looked quickly around the apartment. The air seemed to become thicker and then she heard a soft clicking of metal. She turned sharply around. The sound came from the front door. She took three steps back as the doorknob slowly began to turn. She pressed against the wall and peered around the corner.

Maggie entered the apartment followed by the same Regulators who had been at the coroner's office.

Catty jerked her head back and covered her

mouth as an involuntary gasp came from her throat.

"Come in then," Maggie spoke in a dry voice. Catty didn't detect any fear in her speech. "It will only be a moment."

Maggie's footsteps started down the short hallway, the three Regulators following silently. It would only be seconds before she turned and saw Catty.

Catty glanced quickly around, looking for a place to hide. They were so close now, she could hear the labored breathing of one of the Regulators. She hurried toward a corridor that led from the living room. She waited there and tried to regain her composure.

The air around her began to prickle with the feel of static electricity.

She would have to time-travel if she was going to escape, but she didn't know if she could focus her thoughts. She pictured the tunnel and tried to concentrate. Power surged in her brain. Her surroundings began to blur and waver as her eyes dilated. She glanced down at her watch. The hand started to move backward. She felt relief flow through her and then suddenly the hands on her watch stopped. She blinked, then concentrated and tried again. Her head throbbed, but nothing happened.

"Damn," she muttered and took three long breaths to calm herself and tried again. But all she succeeded in doing was giving herself a head-ache.

She had to do something. A sound made her alert. Was one of them coming to the corridor? She glanced warily at a closed door. She didn't know Maggie's apartment, but whatever lay inside couldn't be as dangerous as waiting until she was discovered.

She put her hand on the knob, twisted it cautiously, and winced as the spring latch scraped softly. With great care, she pushed the door opened, entered the room, and closed it behind her.

The room was empty except for a small ornately carved table in the corner. The manu-script sat on top of the table. She walked over to it and picked it up.

She was deep in thought when behind her, she heard the soft sound of a latch releasing. She dropped the manuscript, jerked around, and stared at the turning doorknob.

CHAPTER FIFTEEN

RESIGNED, CATTY WATCHED the door slowly open.

No one was there.

She let out a sigh of relief. Maybe a draft had opened the door or perhaps she hadn't closed it securely.

She leaned back against the wall and then watched in amazement as the door languidly swung shut.

A dusty cloud formed in front of her, then thickened. Vanessa became visible.

"Vanessa," Catty whispered in astonishment.

"What are you doing here?"

Vanessa glanced cautiously at the door, then walked over to Catty and spoke in hushed tones. "We've been watching you."

"We?"

"Serena read your mind last night at the party," Vanessa continued in a low voice. "She knew you'd decided to sneak into Maggie's apartment to steal back the manuscript. So we decided we'd try to talk you out of it. I called this morning but I guess you'd already left to come here."

Catty remembered Vanessa's early-morning call. "But why did you sneak inside the apartment?" Catty asked. "Don't you know how risky that was?"

"Just as we drove up we saw Maggie and the Regulators." Vanessa nervously brushed her hands through her hair. "We knew if you were inside, you were going to be in big trouble."

Catty looked at her friend with appreciation. "Let's get out of here then. Do you think you can make me invisible?"

"I'll do my best."

Catty walked over to the table and picked up the manuscript. "You'll have to make this invisible, too." Catty held it up. "No way am I leaving it here for Maggie to give to the Regulators."

"I can't believe she'd actually betray us." Vanessa said sadly. "Well, at least we know."

Vanessa put both arms around Catty. Almost immediately the change started. Soon, Catty's feet, legs, and arms elongated and became like clouds of coarse sand. Then she disappeared entirely. She felt Vanessa lightly guiding her, but it was more a sensation of the softest breeze. She loved the lightness of being invisible and the way she could float on the air or spin and twirl with a breeze.

They stopped at the door. Vanessa had learned how to move objects while she was invisible. The door swung open and then they flowed from the room into the corridor.

She followed Vanessa up to the ceiling, and they fluttered over the heads of Maggie and the Regulators.

Catty could feel Vanessa's heartbeat accelerate.

The Regulators seemed suddenly tense and alert as if they could hear it.

She felt the pull of gravity and then she knew what was happening. Vanessa had become too nervous again.

Catty looked in front of her. Vanessa was becoming dense.

Then she glanced down sharply. The molecules of her hand were swirling into formation. Any second she would become too heavy for Vanessa to hold and she'd fall, right on top of the Regulators.

Her molecules began to connect one by one. If the Regulators happened to look up, they'd see a hazy partially formed girl floating above them.

She felt Vanessa tug at her, and then she sensed herself tumbling, head over heels. When she was able to look up again she was at the door, her molecules re-forming rapidly.

"What's that?" one of the Regulators asked.

"What?" Maggie's voice seemed unperturbed. "I didn't hear anything."

A chair pushed back. "Yes, something at the

door. I'll see what it was."

Then another chair scraped back. "I'll check," Maggie announced. "This is an apartment building after all. Noises aren't that unusual."

Maggie's footsteps sounded on the floor.

Catty froze. "Do something!"

"I'm trying," Vanessa shot back in a low voice.

"Come on," Catty glanced down. She was no more than a cloud of dancing dust. She tried to concentrate to make herself invisible again, but it was no use. It required Vanessa's power.

As Maggie turned the corner, Vanessa opened the door a crack and she and Catty rippled outside onto the balcony.

The door started to swing open behind them, and Catty's heart sunk. They were completely solid now and there was nowhere to hide. They couldn't even pretend that they had just stopped by to visit, because Catty held the manuscript in her hands.

CHAPTER SIXTEEN

*S*UDDENLY, VANESSA grabbed Catty and plunged over the railing. Startled, Catty clutched for the iron banister. She caught a handful of ivy and fell. Just as she was about to scream, her molecules spread and melded with the air. Invisible again, she and Vanessa swirled up in a lazy curl, then drifted gently down and landed safely on the ground.

Vanessa dropped her hold and Catty's molecules collided together in icy pain. The manuscript flapped crazily in her hands as tiny specks pulled tightly into place.

"Sorry." Vanessa rubbed her arms.

Catty looked back up at the balcony. "Don't ever do that again," she said in a raspy voice.

"I had no choice," Vanessa answered, looking somewhat pleased with her powers. "Did you want Maggie to see you?"

"What if you hadn't made us invisible in time?" Catty pointed out. "We'd be splattered all over the patio."

Vanessa had a smug smile on her face. "But I *did* make us invisible in time." Then her smile faded. "What are we going to do about Maggie?

Catty shook her head. "I don't know."

Vanessa started walking. "We better tell Jimena and Serena."

They went outside, then turned the corner. Jimena was resting on the hood of the car. Serena was pacing on the sidewalk.

"Well?" Jimena sat up.

Vanessa shook her head. "It's not good news."

Jimena jumped off the car. She and Serena gathered close around Vanessa and Catty, and listened as they explained what had happened inside.

"Why do you think Regulators are with Maggie?" Jimena asked. "Was she really going to give them the manuscript?"

"Yes," Vanessa answered.

"Let's go," Catty interrupted. She had a chilling sense that something bad would happen if they stayed. "Let's go someplace safer before we discuss it more."

She closed her eyes and let a breeze curl around her. She didn't detect any electrical charge in the air, not yet anyway.

They piled into Jimena's car and drove away.

Twenty minutes later, they sat in Catty's kitchen, staring down at the manuscript.

"Any ideas?" Catty asked again.

Serena shook her head. Vanessa sighed.

"I think we need to clear our minds for a while," Jimena said suddenly. "Let's go to Planet Bang and forget about the manuscript for now."

"But what about Maggie?" Vanessa asked.

"It's not like we're coming up with any

brilliant ideas here," Serena remarked.

Catty ran her finger along the edge of the Scroll. "How can I follow the Path of the manuscript, when I can't even read it?"

"Maybe that's what Maggie was supposed to do," Jimena pointed out. "Maybe she was supposed to translate it for you."

"But look at what she did." Vanessa complained.

Catty studied the curling letters. "The answers are all here. All we have to do is find another person to translate it."

"What about Kendra?" Vanessa asked.

Catty felt uneasy. "Do you think it's safe? What about the curse?"

"You don't really believe in the curse, do you?" Jimena asked.

"It's just superstition," Serena put in.

"You're probably right," Catty agreed. "I'll leave it here for Kendra."

"Let's dress up and make it over to Planet Bang." Jimena urged as if she were trying to lift everyone's spirits.

Vanessa hesitated. "I don't know. Toby might—"

"Toby might what?" Serena interrupted with a teasing voice.

Vanessa shrugged.

Catty glanced at Vanessa. Why was she acting so serious? Was she that concerned about upsetting Toby?

Vanessa smiled. "You're right. Let's go!"

Then they all stared at Catty.

"What?" she asked.

"Can we raid Kendra's closet?" Jimena asked.

Catty looked at her friends. Kendra had saved everything from her hippie and disco days. The closets in the spare bedroom were full of her old clothes. She never seemed to mind when Catty and Vanessa borrowed her things. Her clothes fit them nicely. Even though she was tall, she had been extremely thin when she was young, and they could wear most everything in the closet.

"Why not?" Catty laughed.

When they finished dressing, Jimena wore

racy red hot pants, a silky blouse with a star-burst pattern, and crazy ankle boots with thin chains draped around her ankles.

"Too cool." Serena admired Jimena's outfit, then she twirled to show off her own shoulder-baring top that exposed her midriff. She had pasted a crystal in her belly button. Kendra's bell-bottoms had been too long, but when she stepped into a pair of gold '70s platform shoes the length became just right.

Catty wore a backless halter top and a pair of lacy bell-bottoms. She held up some stencils. "Kendra is going to start selling these at the shop. Anyone want to try one?" She had two dragons in one hand and a lacy snowflake pattern in the other.

Jimena and Serena started to examine them, when Vanessa walked into the room. She was wearing a pinstripe shirt unbuttoned over a black leather bra top. Kendra's mini-skirt was too big and the waist fell around Vanessa's hips. Her skin looked golden bronze and she had applied one of the snowflake stencils on her stomach.

"Wow," Serena said.

"Talk about going for the jugular," Jimena teased.

"You like it?" she asked and took off the shirt. "It's too hot to wear." She hung it back on a hanger.

"Let's go, then." Jimena started for the door.

The strobe light flashed and blue lasers swept over the girls as they entered Planet Bang. The club was crowded already. The DJ turned the music and a loud beat vibrated through the haze.

A hand touched Catty's back. She turned quickly. Chris stood behind her. He smiled at her and she liked the feel of his hand on her bare back.

"Let's dance," he whispered.

She nodded.

He took her hand, but instead of taking her out to the dance floor he pulled her back to the shadows.

Catty stopped. "Why do you want to dance over here?"

He leaned next to her. "I don't want to share you with anyone."

She smiled back at him and followed him into a far corner. Both his hands held her waist, and a pleasant warmth ran through her body. He danced slow against her and stared down at her, his eyes lingering on her lips. She parted her mouth slightly and waited.

"You look so beautiful, Catty." His eyes did not leave hers. "I wish we could be together always."

His fingers wandered up her back and rested on her shoulders, then he cupped her face in his hands and bent down. He gave her a light kiss and murmured against her, "I like you a lot, Catty. Always believe that, even if I act strangely. It doesn't have anything to do with the way I feel about you. That's real. I just have a lot going on right now that I can't talk about."

He pulled away and she stared back at him, feeling suddenly guilty. So many kids had bad things going on in their lives. She wondered if his parents were going through a divorce or having money problems.

"I'm here for you if you want to talk," she offered. "Anytime. Just call me or come over."

"Thanks." His hands brushed down her arms and he pulled her tight against him.

She closed her eyes and let her arms slowly wrap around his neck. She had never imagined that it could feel this good to dance with a guy. Her lips moved across his cheek, searching for his. She needed a kiss. Then his lips found hers and softly traced the outline of her mouth. His kiss tasted even sweeter than she remembered and the feel of his hands on her back made her light-headed and breathless.

They stood motionless in the shadows, and then she felt him pull back. She didn't want him to stop.

"Promise you'll trust me," he whispered. "Promise, no matter what happens."

She nodded. How could she not trust him? And yet the way he was asking made her think that something really bad had happened to him or his family. And then she realized with a shock that she had never heard him mention his parents or any brothers or sisters.

"Maybe we should go someplace and talk," she suggested.

She felt him shake his head, then he leaned in to kiss her again when a commotion made them turn.

Michael was dancing with Vanessa, and Toby was picking a fight with him.

"What's he doing now?" Catty asked and started to run over to find out what was going on.

Chris grabbed her arm and pulled her back. "Who's the guy with Michael?"

Chris's eyes held hers and he pointed behind her. "That guy. He doesn't go to our school. Who is he?"

"You're right," Catty answered and wondered why Chris would care. "That's Toby. He goes to Fairfax High, I think. I'm not really sure. He's some guy that Vanessa met in dance class."

She thought he would let her go now, but he didn't. His hand squeezed tighter and he stared at Toby as if he sensed something.

"I have to help Vanessa." Catty started to pull away. "Come on, Toby is just a hundred percent creep."

She ran out to the dance floor, expecting Chris to follow her. She pushed through the ring of kids who had circled Toby, Michael, and Vanessa. She reached a hand back for Chris, but he wasn't there. She didn't see him anywhere. Where had he gone? She didn't have time to look for him now.

Toby glared at Michael.

"Toby?" Vanessa grabbed his arm as he started to lunge forward. "Stop. You want to get us kicked out?"

Toby laughed and the sound made Catty's scalp tingle.

Suddenly he charged forward and swung at Michael. Michael ducked, and Toby lost his balance.

Kids laughed at his clumsiness. Toby looked enraged.

Michael put both hands up and shook his head. "Vanessa and I are just friends, okay? I only asked a friend to dance."

Toby answered with a shove at Michael's chest. Michael took two quick steps backward to regain his balance, then shrugged and smiled crookedly. Catty could tell he was starting to become angry and that was dangerous.

"Sorry," Michael said sarcastically. "I didn't know you were so insecure about Vanessa. I thought things were solid between the two of you."

Toby started to swing, but Jimena suddenly appeared from the crowd and grabbed his wrist. He turned, ready to fight. But she tilted her head in a flirty way and smiled up at him as only Jimena could do.

"Stop making an ass of yourself," she whispered in a coy voice. "He just danced with her. You want to get a reputation for being weak?"

Toby glanced at Michael, then back at Jimena.

She leaned in close to him, a hand on her hip. "Yeah, if you believe your girl is yours, then there's no way some *vato* is going to steal her love with a dance. *No seas un payaso.*"

Toby seemed to understand everything she was saying. He considered Jimena, then glanced at Vanessa. Abruptly he took Vanessa's hand, smiled, and pulled her tightly against his chest. She gazed up in his eyes, and they started dancing as if nothing had happened.

Catty stared in amazement. "Can't she see how gross he is?"

"Love is blind," Michael said grimly.

Serena shook her head. "Are you okay, Michael?"

He looked at her. "I'm fine. I never would have asked Vanessa to dance if I'd known Toby would freak out."

Jimena shook her head. "Why did he get so mad?"

"Because," Catty explained, "Vanessa still likes Michael and he knows it."

Michael tossed his head and shook the wild black curls away from his face. "You couldn't tell by the way she's acting." He had a wounded look on his face.

"I know she does," Catty assured him.

He shrugged and grabbed Serena's hand as the beat of the music changed. A spark flew between them. Michael looked surprised, then smiled at Serena. "Let's dance." They walked out to the dance floor. Jimena began dancing with them.

Catty watched for a moment, then looked around the room, wondering where Chris had gone. She sighed heavily. She didn't see him anywhere and she didn't want to stay alone. She walked outside, hoping she might find him there. A long line of kids was still waiting to go inside.

The moon was high in the night sky, and she decided against taking the bus. She turned down a side street and started the long walk home.

A breeze soughed through the palm trees overhead. The night air felt cool against her face. She thought of Chris and wondered what had happened to him. She wished he would talk to her. Problems were always easier to bear when they were shared.

On the opposite side of the street, the trees blocked the light, making the shadows dense and thick. As she stepped onto the sidewalk, she heard something that made her stop and turn. It sounded like a footstep.

Her body felt suddenly tense and watchful. She looked behind her. The road was empty. Maybe it had only been someone walking around their house, taking out the trash or fixing a water sprinkler. She shrugged and began walking again, but now an odd sensation overcame her. Someone was following her.

She slowed her steps and wondered if it could be the guy who had given her the manuscript.

"Hello," she called and turned slowly, watching for any movement in the shadows around her.

Silence answered her.

She waited, hoping that if it were the mystery man he would step forward and show himself. She wanted to meet him, to see his face, and ask him about the manuscript.

"I know you're there," she spoke softly. "I can feel your presence."

Again silence answered her.

Finally she started walking, her shoes tapping nicely on the cement walk.

When she got to her house, she unlocked the door and entered, then without turning on the lights, she tiptoed to the picture window in the front room and looked out, searching for whoever had followed her home. Disappointed, she turned and walked through the dark house to the kitchen. She was about to switch on the light, when she sensed someone in the room with her.

CHAPTER SEVENTEEN

KENDRA SAT AT THE kitchen table, holding the manuscript. She stared silently at Catty with the wide-eyed look of an insomniac. Her hair was wet and matted against her skull as if she were burning with a high fever. Beads of sweat clung to her upper lip.

The manuscript fluttered in her hands. Kendra was shaking too violently to hold it steady.

"You," Kendra whispered.

"Are you all right?" Catty asked, taking a step forward. Kendra looked seriously ill.

Kendra stood abruptly. Her chair fell back and crashed to the floor. She stepped around it and eased to the back of the kitchen. Her eyes never left Catty.

"Kendra, what's wrong?" Catty started for her again, but stopped when she realized Kendra was afraid of her.

"I finished translating it." Kendra tapped the manuscript. "And now I know the truth."

"The truth about what?"

Kendra held the manuscript up and it flapped in her hands. *"Demere personam tuam atque ad dominum tuum se referre!"* she shouted roughly.

Catty stared at her in disbelief. She knew the words were Latin. She repeated the sound of the words to herself, trying to find their meaning. "Day-mair-eh pear-so-nahm too-ahm aht-kweh ahd dom-in-oom too-oom say reh-fair-reh."

Kendra seemed empowered when she spoke the words. She repeated them, the words scraping from her throat. *"Demere personam tuam atque ad dominum tuum se referre."*

Catty was totally confused now. "Take off

my mask? Return to my master? What's that supposed to mean?"

Kendra collapsed against the back wall. Silent tears rolled down her cheeks. "Who are you?" she asked in a low voice.

Catty shook her head. "I don't understand."

"What are you?" Kendra demanded.

Catty didn't know what to say.

Kendra's head lolled against the wall. Her eyes were only half-open. "All these years I thought I had been protecting a space alien from the government." She laughed and it was dry and filled with sadness. "And now I find out that I've been protecting something evil."

Catty started shaking. "What did you read?"

Kendra looked down at the manuscript. Her finger ran across a line as she translated it. *"The child of a fallen goddess and an evil spirit will take possession of the Secret Scroll without fear of its curse."*

"You think that's me?" Catty asked nervously. Could she be the daughter of a fallen goddess and an evil spirit?

Catty slumped into a chair and stared at

nothing. "I'm not evil. I'm a goddess," she confessed softly. "I didn't know until this year. When I found out, I tried to tell you. I started to tell you." Her voice trailed off.

Kendra dragged a chair to the table and sat down facing Catty.

"Tell me now." Kendra started to shiver again but Catty suspected that this time it was from fever, not fear.

Right now, sitting across from Kendra, Catty believed that the manuscript did have a curse and she had to do something to find out how to free Kendra from its spell.

Catty began slowly, repeating what Maggie had told her. "In ancient times when Pandora's box was opened—"

"Pandora?" Kendra interrupted. "Are you talking about the myth?"

Catty nodded solemnly. "It isn't a myth," she stated firmly and continued, "The last thing to leave the box was hope. Only Selene, the goddess of the moon, saw the creature that had been sent by the Atrox to devour hope. Selene took pity on the people of earth and gave her Daughters, like guardian angels, to perpetuate hope. I'm one of those Daughters. A goddess."

"And the Atrox?" Kendra asked.

"The Atrox and its Followers have sworn to destroy the Daughters of the Moon because once we're gone, the Atrox will succeed." She looked at Kendra. "I'm a source of good."

Kendra's lips trembled. Her eyes searched over the text of the manuscript and then she found what she was looking for and translated, *"A soulless creature who defied God and gave itself life."* Her voice seemed haunted. *"The Atrox."*

The room suddenly felt crowded with hostile forces as if saying its name had summoned it. The temperature dropped, and a chill tingled up Catty's spine.

"And your gift?" It seemed to pain Kendra to speak.

"It's not teleportation. It's a form of time travel. It's part of what I need to fight the Atrox," Catty explained.

"An entity that has existed since before

creation." Kendra spoke more to herself than to Catty. "And this." She held the manuscript more tightly. "This tells how to destroy it, and . . ." She looked back at Catty now. "You're the one chosen to destroy it."

Catty nodded, then looked down self-consciously.

Kendra regarded her in admiration. "What can I do to help?"

"I need to see my mother," Catty started. "I need to go back in time before her death and talk to her so that I can find out who my father is and why I was the one given the manuscript." She didn't add that she hoped her mother would also know how to free Kendra from the curse.

Kendra nodded and stood on shaky feet, set the Scroll on her chair, then walked slowly to the kitchen cupboard where she kept messages, notes, and telephone numbers. She pulled out a scrap of paper. When she turned back, her eyes held Catty's. "It's the curse of the manuscript, isn't it? That's why I'm so ill."

"No," Catty lied. "I'm sure it's the just the

flu. You don't believe in curses anyway, do you?" She tried to laugh but it sounded forced.

Kendra smiled weakly. "I do now." She handed the piece of paper to Catty. "This is the address the coroner's office gave me."

She leaned back against the counter as if standing for such a short time had weakened her.

Catty prayed that she had enough time. "Maybe I should take you to the doctor before I go," she offered.

Kendra shook her head. "I don't think modern medicine can cure what I have." Her hand touched Catty's cheek and her tired eyes filled with love. "I'll have to rely on you, Catty." She hesitated a moment. "And to think that all this time I thought you were a space alien."

"No regrets?" Catty asked.

"Of course I have regrets." Kendra tried to chuckle but burst into a hacking cough. Finally she was able to speak again. "I had always hoped you were going to take me to another planet someday so I could see what outer space really looked like."

She leaned over and kissed Catty's cheek. Her skin felt too hot and dry.

Catty watched Kendra wave good-bye as a glaring white explosion burned the kitchen away and Catty zoomed into the tunnel at a speed faster than light.

CHAPTER EIGHTEEN

CATTY RECOGNIZED THE street with all the magnolia trees and suddenly she became aware of how close her mother had lived to her all these years. The knowledge filled her with deep sadness and longing. She stopped in front of a narrow house with a pitched roof, took a deep breath, and headed up the brick path. Roses in every color lined the walkway and perfumed the night with their sweet fragrance. A rake rested on the porch step next to a paper bag filled with leaves and a pair of gardening gloves. Catty knocked on the door hesitantly, then rang the doorbell.

The door opened with a suddenness that surprised her. A hand reached out, grabbed her wrist, and pulled her inside.

Catty started to speak but warm fingers pressed against her lips to silence her. The sudden touch surprised her.

"Mom?" she whispered.

"Yes," Zoe whispered back. Her hand lingered on Catty's lips and the touch brought tears to Catty's eyes.

Zoe switched off the lights before she pulled Catty into the living room.

"Stay here," she ordered softly. She walked to the picture window and held back the lace panel with the side of her hand. She studied the outside for a long time, then finally satisfied, she drew the drapes, turned on a small lamp, and sat on a sofa filled with quilted pillows. She smiled at Catty. She had a pretty smile.

"So," she said quietly. "I'm sorry for the intrigue. There are Regulators watching me from the corner house. I guess they think their disguise has fooled me. I had to make sure they hadn't seen you come here. Very sloppy of them not to have seen you turn the corner."

"I didn't come *that way*," Catty answered.

"No?" Zoe patted the sofa for Catty to sit next to her. "Of course not. You have special powers of your own."

Catty started to join her, but then she looked down and saw the geometry test she had hurriedly written on and given to Zoe that day on the desert.

Zoe caught her look and picked up the test from the coffee table. "I always keep it with me," she explained. "It's the only thing of yours I own." She folded it gently and tucked it in her pocket. "Besides, I can't chance having a Regulator discover it."

"Don't they know where I live already since I'm a Daughter?" Catty wondered.

"Possibly," Zoe answered. "But I'm sure they don't know you're *my* daughter or you wouldn't be here."

Catty felt a chill run up her back.

"Right now they may think it's Serena or Jimena or not have a clue at all. They're extremely evil and powerful, but putting so much energy into their disguise makes them a bit sluggish sometimes."

Catty hated to think what one of the Regulators would be like without a disguise but then she thought of something else. "You know about Serena and Jimena?"

"Yes, I know most everything about your life."

A warm feeling spread through Catty's chest. "Everything?"

"All that I could learn." She smiled, then became serious and continued. "So I suppose something important has happened for you to find me? Who told you where I live?"

Catty sat down and started to tell her but stopped. How could she explain to her that she had gotten the address from the coroner's office?

"So you can't tell me," Zoe concluded. "Or won't, because it's something I shouldn't know or wouldn't want to know." She shrugged. "But you can at least tell me why you are here."

"I've received the Secret Scroll." Catty's voice

caught. "I was hoping you could explain why all this is happening to me. Why was I given the Scroll? I can't even read it."

Zoe leaned back on a pillow and looked at the ceiling. "I had planned on telling you before now. I should have but I was too ashamed."

Catty cast a brief look at Zoe. "Ashamed of what?"

"I had been a Daughter of the Moon like you. I had a special power, too. I could move objects with my mind." Zoe's words seemed filled with regret. "But I became too frightened of the change."

Catty nodded. She didn't like to think about the change. Their gifts only lasted until they were seventeen and then there was metamorphosis. They lost their powers and their memory of what they had been, or they disappeared. The ones who disappeared became something else but no one, not even Maggie, knew what that was.

She continued softly. "So I turned to the Atrox."

Catty's eyes widened.

Zoe drew her moon amulet from beneath her blouse for Catty to see. It still looked dull and blackened.

"The Atrox promised to give me immortality," she continued. "But it tricked me. I had failed to ask for perpetual youth and now I'm doomed to age for eternity. It's not a problem now but eventually . . . Can you imagine what it will feel like to continue aging until the end of time?"

Catty shook her head.

"The Atrox must have sensed that I made my commitment out of fear." Zoe stared off for a long while, then finally she spoke again. "That day on the desert, I was still blaming Maggie for what had happened to me. I thought for a long time that if Maggie could have told me more about the transformation, then I wouldn't have been afraid and I wouldn't have turned to the Atrox. But I know now that it was my own lack of courage that made me do what I did. I wish I had listened to her." Zoe shrugged. "But then maybe all things have a purpose."

She stared at Catty and Catty could tell from the look in her eyes that she didn't want to hear what she was going to say next.

"You never would have come into the world if I hadn't become a Follower," Zoe uttered softly.

"I don't understand." Catty tried to catch her breath.

"I fell in love with a Follower." Zoe smiled sadly. "A member of the Inner Circle."

Catty felt devastated. "But members of the Inner Circle are renowned for their evil." She tried to keep her voice steady but the words felt like bricks falling from her tongue. "They're incapable of loving."

"Yes," Zoe agreed. "But they're also very seductive and captivating."

"Who?" The simple question scraped from her throat. Did she really want to know?

Zoe stared at her as if considering, then she shook her head slightly. "You'll know who your father is only when it is essential for you to find out."

Catty could feel hot tears pressing into her

eyes. She fought to keep them from rolling down her cheeks.

Zoe continued. "I feared that you were the destined heir to the Secret Scroll because of the prophecy."

"What prophecy?" Catty hated the tremor that had crept into her voice.

"Only the child of a fallen goddess and an evil spirit will inherit the Scroll," Zoe recited.

Catty's heart sunk. Her mother was a Follower, her father an evil member of the Inner Circle. She suddenly felt damned. How could she overcome such a birthright?

Zoe took Catty's hand. "You must never worry that you are evil because of your heritage. The manuscript can only be given to someone with a pure heart and the strength to fight the Atrox."

Catty looked at Zoe's hand holding her own. Finally she had the courage to ask her the question that had been bothering her all these years. "Why did you leave me by the side of the road?"

Zoe waited a long moment before she

answered. "It was the only way I could think of to save you."

Catty looked up at her and saw that Zoe's eyes were shimmering with tears.

"When I heard about the legend of the Secret Scroll, I assumed that you were its heir. I couldn't know for sure but I lived in terror. I feared that if you were given the manuscript, the Atrox would destroy you and the Scroll. I had to do something. I would have preferred to never see you again and know you were safe than to let the Atrox have you. So I abandoned you. I crashed the car and set it on fire, planning to say that I had lost consciousness and that you must have wandered off."

"But in the desert," Catty said accusingly, "I could have died so easily."

Zoe reassured her. "I assumed that anyone seeing a child walking along the road in a deserted stretch of highway would stop." Then she quickly added, "Besides, you know that I was watching over you until someone did stop."

"But why didn't the Regulators find me?

They could have found me through my dreams."
She stopped. She was remembering what her
mother had said to Stanton that day in the desert.
She had begged him to take Catty's memories
from her so she'd be safe.

"That's right," Zoe said as if she understood
what Catty was thinking. "Without your memories, it would be hard for the Regulators to find
you and destroy you."

"But you didn't know Stanton would show
up."

"No, I didn't. Until he showed up my plan
was risky, I know, but I'd hoped that if a stranger
reared you, you'd be safe. I hadn't counted on
Stanton. I don't have the powers he has. I knew
then that my plan might work. Without memories
for the Regulators to explore, they wouldn't be
able to find you."

Catty suddenly understood that Stanton had
saved her. It was hard for her to imagine that he
would do anything to help her. "Why would
Stanton help me?"

"You don't understand how valuable the

Secret Scroll is and how many people want it," Zoe answered. "I'm sure he hoped that if he took you back in time to see me that I would convince you to give the manuscript to him."

"But you didn't."

"No." Zoe brushed her hand against Catty's cheek.

"I'll find a way to release you from what the Atrox has done to you," Catty promised suddenly.

"It's too late for that," Zoe acknowledged.

"Let me try at least," Catty urged. "I know I can do something."

Zoe shook her head. "I've been dreaming about the goddess Selene. She comes to me in my dreams and offers me a second chance because I've done so much to protect you."

"Are you going to accept her offer?" Catty instantly felt reassured.

"Yes." Zoe nodded.

"Then why haven't you?"

"Because I know that when I accept her offer, I'll leave this body behind and become something different. I've only been waiting to talk to you again before I go."

Catty looked at Zoe and felt a terrible ache and yearning. "Why didn't you ever try to see me? You live so close. It hurts to know you were always right here and never even called me."

"I did see you," Zoe confessed. "When it was safe and I knew the Regulators weren't following me, I watched you. Sometimes I was even bold enough to go into your room at night and sit by your bed. I would speak to you while you were sleeping."

Catty was startled and wondered if the presence she had sometimes felt had been her mother.

"I'm sure I'll be able to continue to visit you after." Zoe grinned. "But you won't be able to see me. I think of how much I feared the transition when I was young, but now I'm eager for it. I think we become guardian spirits so I'll always be watching over you." Zoe stood abruptly. "I'm ready." She held out her hand. "Stay with me until Selene comes."

Catty stood and followed Zoe through a

back bedroom to a door that led to a small enclosed garden. Catty saw a small ornate mirror on the dresser. She wanted to have something that had belonged to her mother. She slipped it into her pocket, then held her hand protectively against it.

They sat outside in the backyard. They hadn't been there long when the lunar glow began to brighten. Soon an eerie whiteness covered the lawn. A blazing light stretched from the moon and Zoe lifted her hand as if she could see something in the frosty beam. When her hand fell back, the light twirled up and up, scattering stars.

Then the yard was dark again and only her mother's body remained.

CHAPTER NINETEEN

CATTY RETURNED TO the present. She dropped from the tunnel back into time and landed hard in the geranium bed at the side of her house. She jumped up, brushed the dirt and petals from her clothes, and started walking to the back of her house. She wanted nothing more than to climb in bed and sleep. She felt exhausted.

She took one step forward and felt a hand touch her gently.

"Catty." The voice of the mysterious stranger made her stop.

"What now?" She didn't bother to hide the irritation in her voice.

"Why are you delaying?" His tone sounded urgent.

"The Scroll has a curse," Catty reminded him and slipped her hand into her pocket. She curled her fingers around the mirror she had taken from the dresser in her mother's house.

"Every second you delay gives the Atrox more of a chance to find the Scroll."

"It's not as simple as you make it sound," Catty responded angrily and slowly inched the mirror from her pocket.

"It is your destiny as heir." His voice sounded as angry as hers now.

"Well, it's not exactly as if I'm not trying," Catty answered and eased the mirror upward. "But I've had to deal with Regulators and the death of my birth mother."

Abruptly she brought the mirror up high enough to see the reflection of the person who stood behind her. She gasped and quickly turned. "Chris?" Her heart beat so rapidly she thought it would leave her body. She dropped the mirror back in her pocket. She felt totally confused, now. How could Chris be the one who had given her the Secret Scroll?

Then she started laughing. She felt mentally exhausted and supertired. No way was Chris the mysterious stranger. She must have misunderstood what he had said to her or maybe she had even fallen asleep in the geraniums and he had just now awakened her.

But when Chris spoke she knew with certainty that she had not been dreaming.

"I guess I'm glad I don't have to pretend anymore." His real voice was neither the one Chris had used with her before, or that of the mysterious stranger, but a pleasant tone in between. "It's been really hard."

She shook her head. Her thoughts whirled. Could it be true? "You gave me the Secret Scroll?"

He nodded.

"Why didn't you just hand it to me?" Catty asked with mounting exasperation. "Why all the mystery?"

"I had to hide who I really was," Chris insisted. "So I could succeed in accomplishing the task I have been ordained to do."

Catty folded her arms over her chest. "Which is?"

"To protect the Scroll," Chris explained. "The Keeper must always hide his identity."

"Keeper?"

Chris stepped closer to her. "The one who protects the manuscript until it can be given to the heir."

She exhaled. "I believed your act. You convinced me and my friends."

His hand went up and gently touched her cheek. "I hated deceiving you, Catty. I really care about you. You gave me back emotions I hadn't felt in years."

She felt her heart skid away from her.

"What is it?" He seemed to sense her distress.

She cocked her head and stared at him. "You're not just some guy I'm going to go to the prom with, are you?"

He shook his head.

"Why did you let me like you then?" She hated how desperate her voice sounded.

His hands rested on her shoulders and even in the faint lighting she could see the regret in his eyes. "I didn't mean for it to happen this way. When I first met you I had no idea you were the one I'd be giving the Scroll to."

"Why not?"

"Normally, I know who is going to be heir to the Scroll from the moment of their birth, but when your mother hid you from the Regulators she also hid you from me."

"But you're in Los Angeles now," she stated. "Why did you come here?"

"I discovered that Maggie was in Los Angeles, so I assumed the Daughters were also here. When I saw the four of you go into Maggie's apartment, I knew one of you was the heir, but that was already after I had met you. I really liked you. I still do, but I couldn't chance having the Regulators see us together."

Then another thought came to her and she

pulled back. "Is this the way you really look or have I been kissing some decrepit old man?"

He laughed. "No, this is me."

At least she hadn't been kissing some old geezer. She sighed.

"What?" he asked and pulled her closer to him.

"I'm living in a nightmare," she answered. "And it just keeps getting worse."

"I'm sorry. It's my fault. I knew I had to give up seeing you for the sake of the manuscript but I couldn't. I never thought I would feel what it's like to be in love again."

She looked up at him, startled. Had he said *in love?* She couldn't control the foolish smile spreading across her cheeks.

"Maybe we can be together someday," he whispered.

"Someday?" she asked.

"You don't stay in this form forever," he said. "And if the Atrox is defeated . . ." He didn't complete the sentence. He leaned forward and started to press his lips against hers.

"If the Atrox is defeated what?" she asked, her lips brushing the words against his mouth.

"Then we can be together." He started to press against her but pulled back suddenly. "You're too young to understand how much you mean to me."

"Well, I'm not centuries old yet," she added defensively.

"Not yet," he chuckled and pulled her close against him.

He felt like flesh and bone. She opened her eyes. His skin looked young. His eyes were bright and clear.

"Have you finished checking?" he asked, his breath caressing her cheeks.

She closed her eyes and he kissed her. She parted her lips and felt his tongue brush lightly against hers. She leaned against him, forgetting all her problems and let herself feel the comfort of his arms around her. Maybe everything would turn out all right.

And then Chris reluctantly released her. "I can't stay with you, Catty. The Regulators don't know who I am yet, and they don't know for sure which one of you is the heir. It's safer if we don't see each other for now."

He walked backward until he was at the corner of the house, then he turned and walked away.

She felt suddenly optimistic, better than she had in days. With a sudden impulse she decided to share the news about Chris with Vanessa. Everything was going to work out now. She was sure of it.

CHAPTER TWENTY

CATTY RAN INSIDE and checked on Kendra. She was sleeping, a bottle of aspirin beside her bed. "You're going to be all right, Kendra," Catty promised her. "I know I'll find a way to help you." She kissed her forehead. The skin felt hot and dry. She took another blanket from the closet and placed it around Kendra, then she called a cab.

Twenty minutes later, she was running up the walk to Vanessa's small Craftsman-style house. She hurried past the twisted olive tree in the front yard and went around to the back. Even before she opened the door, she could smell popcorn.

She walked in, calling Vanessa's name.

"It's me, Vanessa," she called. "Please be home."

Vanessa crossed the kitchen. Normally, a smile burst across her face when she saw Catty, but her face seemed solemn. Her hair was tangled, and she was rubbing her eyes.

"Something wrong?" Catty asked and pinched a kernel of popcorn from the bowl on the table. She threw it up in the air and caught it with her mouth.

Vanessa smiled sluggishly. "I must have fallen asleep on the couch."

"Guess what?" Catty opened the refrigerator and pulled out a Coke. She popped the top and took a drink.

Vanessa only stared at her.

"Well, you could show some enthusiasm," Catty squealed. "I'm about to tell you one of the most exciting stories of my life!"

"What?" Vanessa was suddenly interested.

"Chris!" Catty shouted. "He's not seeing anyone else."

"I never thought he was," Vanessa answered. "Is that what you came over to tell me?"

"But guess what else?" Catty set the Coke aside. She felt too excited to drink it now.

Vanessa got a surprised look on her face. "You didn't . . ."

"Of course, we didn't," Catty interrupted her and sat down at the table. "This is way more exciting."

Vanessa looked puzzled. She pulled out a chair, sat down, and faced Catty. "More exciting than *that*?"

Catty leaned forward. "He's the mysterious stranger."

A worried look flashed across Vanessa's face and then it was gone. "What do you mean?" she whispered as if she were afraid someone would hear.

"The person who gave me the manuscript," Catty announced. "It was Chris all along."

Vanessa's hand clasped Catty's and her face looked confused as if she were fighting conflicting emotions.

"What's wrong?" Catty turned.

Toby walked quietly into the kitchen, his eyes glaring.

"Do you always listen to private conversations?" Catty practically yelled, then she turned to Vanessa. "You should have told me that Toby was here."

Vanessa didn't respond. She seemed almost unaware that anyone was in the room with them, her eyes were glazed and her mind seemed far away.

Catty glanced back at Toby. He smiled at her smugly. "Now I know who the Keeper is."

Catty felt her heart sink. "A Regulator." As Catty said the word the room seemed to come alive with an electrical charge. The small hairs on her arms and neck rose, and she suddenly understood why she and Jimena and Serena were always getting tiny shocks when Toby was around.

"You liked my disguise?" Toby grinned maliciously and his eyes became clouded, rheumy with age, and yellowed. The skin on his face fell into wrinkles as the flesh turned a sickly green color. His perfectly cut hair grew into thick tangles. But worse was his smell, and the bluish mold that gathered on his clothes and skin.

Catty stood suddenly. The chair legs scraped across the kitchen floor with a horrible scream. She backed away from him. Her hand rose automatically and covered her nose.

"Now you two can see the real me." His mouth stretched into a ghoulish wound and his fingers grew longer, the nails yellowing and splitting.

Toby crouched over Vanessa, his breathing labored, and kissed the top of her head.

Catty wondered how Vanessa didn't cringe from him. She didn't even seem to notice the way Toby looked now, or his putrid smell.

Toby stood up again, his clawlike hands resting on Vanessa's shoulders. "Vanessa can only see me the way I want her to see me," he bragged in an ugly rasping voice. "I've gone into her dreams every night and influenced all of her thoughts." He patted Vanessa. "You see me as quite charming, don't you, Vanessa?"

Catty felt ill. She looked at Vanessa and

wondered what she could do to save her friend. She felt too rattled to think clearly.

Toby cleared his throat and when she looked back at him, he was again in his high-school-boy disguise.

"I will take care of Chris," he spoke with assurance. "All that remains is for you to destroy the manuscript."

"No chance of that." Catty folded her arms across her chest.

"Is that so?" Toby asked. "All right, then." He turned to Vanessa. "Do you want to go away with me, Vanessa?"

Vanessa stood quickly and placed her arms around him. "Yes," she answered without hesitation, but Catty thought she saw a flicker of doubt cross Vanessa's eyes.

"Come, then." Toby took her hand and started to lead her out the back door.

"Wait!" Catty yelled.

Toby glanced back at her.

"I'll get rid of the manuscript," she offered. "Just let Vanessa stay with me."

"You'll get rid of it?"

She nodded.

He considered her for a long moment.

"Meet me tomorrow night in Griffith Park before the full moon rises. Bring the manuscript with you, and I'll show you how to destroy it."

"Where in the park?" Catty asked.

"Near the carousel." He started to lead Vanessa out the door again.

"Wait." Catty ran after them and grabbed Vanessa's hand. "Vanessa stays with me."

Vanessa cast Catty a strange look and jerked her hand away. "What are you doing, Catty?"

"I want you to stay with me," Catty urged.

"Why?" Vanessa looked perplexed.

Catty grabbed Vanessa and held her tightly. "Please, I'll give you the manuscript right now," Catty told him. "Just let Vanessa stay."

"That's not what I want," he assured her. "The manuscript cannot be destroyed by ordinary means. It can only be destroyed by the destined heir." He looked at her maliciously. "Bring it to the park tomorrow night and then you can have Vanessa back."

Catty nodded her agreement but she knew intuitively that there was no way Toby was going to surrender Vanessa once Catty had surrendered the manuscript. The Regulators would destroy them, or worse, change them both into Followers.

Before she was even aware that she was speaking, words spilled from her mouth. *"O Mater Luna, Regina nocis, adiuvo me nunc."* The prayer was only said in times of grave danger.

Catty watched Vanessa leave. She felt totally hopeless.

CHAPTER TWENTY-ONE

AT HOME, CATTY sat on the front porch steps and gazed up at the western sky. Veils of smoke wreathed around the moon. The fire in the hills behind her home had been contained but a larger one had started in the chaparral in another area.

She didn't see any way to outwit Toby. She thought about calling Serena and Jimena, but that felt too dangerous. She'd only be inviting them to their doom, and she didn't want more people harmed by the manuscript.

Maybe it was best to destroy it. That might

save Chris and Kendra at least. Why would Regulators need to go after Chris if there was no manuscript to protect? And if the manuscript were destroyed, then perhaps Kendra would be free of the curse as well.

The night had fallen quiet but for a fleeting moment, she thought she heard someone call her name. She listened carefully wondering if it was Kendra.

Then soft steps crossed the porch and she turned expecting to see Kendra, but instead a woman walked toward her with slow, easy steps. Was she a neighbor searching for a lost pet? Catty didn't recognize her and she didn't feel like talking with a stranger.

"Can I help you?" Catty asked.

"You help me?" the woman answered and a wry smile crossed her face as if she thought the idea was funny. She sat down on the porch stoop next to Catty and stared up at the moon.

The woman sighed and looked at Catty. "How can you lose hope now, when it is most important?"

Catty shook her head. She didn't know what

the woman was talking about, and just as quickly the woman answered her thoughts.

"You know very well what I'm talking about," the woman said. "That's all you've been thinking."

Catty studied her. She had an inexplicable feeling that the woman sitting beside her wasn't just a neighbor. Serena and Jimena had each told her about visits from a moon goddess when they were desperate. Could the woman beside her be the goddess Selene in disguise? Catty felt a wrinkle of irritation. Her situation really was hopeless. "This is the end," Catty said. "There's no escape. I don't have any choices left."

Again the woman smiled as if she found humor in Catty's answer. "You always have a choice."

"Right," Catty answered sarcastically.

"No situation is ever completely hopeless," the woman insisted. "You're just not seeing the alternatives."

"Get real," Catty said.

"Maybe if you told me your problem—"

"I thought you already knew about my problems," Catty cut in.

"Suit yourself." The woman stood to leave.

Catty sighed heavily and spoke in a weary voice. "I don't even know if the manuscript is worth saving, because it has hurt so many people. It turned Maggie against me, and the curse is so powerful that even the Regulators are afraid to touch it."

The woman sat down again. "Maggie never betrayed you."

"She didn't?" Catty turned sharply and stared at the woman. "How do you know?"

"Trust me." The woman smiled. "Maggie believes in the curse, and she thought she was protecting you."

"But why were the Regulators in her apartment, then?" Catty desperately wanted to believe in Maggie, still. "She was going to give the manuscript to them."

"Yes," the woman nodded. "She wanted to see the manuscript destroyed, so that the Atrox would think it was safe. She didn't know the manuscript could only be destroyed by the heir. If the Atrox believed it was safe, it would be less cautious. Only then would she send her beloved Daughters to fight it."

Catty's heart pounded.

The woman tilted her head and looked at Catty. "Maggie had memorized the Path of the manuscript before she offered to surrender it to the Regulators, but then . . ." Her eyes twinkled and she shrugged. "The manuscript mysteriously disappeared from her apartment."

"I stole it," Catty confessed.

"Of course you did." The woman smiled kindly.

"Did . . . did they harm her?" Catty's voice was shaky and her hands trembled. She couldn't bare it if one more person were harmed because of her stupidity.

"No. After all, she was going to give them the manuscript. They wrongly consider her an ally."

Catty felt relieved. She didn't know what she would have done if the Regulators had hurt

Maggie. The woman glanced at the moon. It was beginning to set. "Well, my time is up." She stood and started to leave, then turned and looked back at Catty. "It's strange," she started.

"What?" Catty asked.

"Just that you've never followed the rules before," the woman explained. "And so now I'm wondering, why are you going to follow them when you are dealing with the most deceitful being in creation?"

Catty watched the woman leave. What she said was true. Catty hated rules.

A slow smile crept across her face.

"Thank you," Catty said. First she'd sleep, and then she'd act.

CHAPTER TWENTY-TWO

THE NEXT MORNING Catty awoke to the sound of sirens and the low rumble of fire trucks speeding down her street. She was surprised she had slept so long. Sunlight slanted through her windows in thick gold bars. She checked on Kendra, showered, and dressed, then crept downstairs to the kitchen. She took down the framed manuscript from the kitchen wall. It was Kendra's prized possession, and part of her felt guilty for what she planned, but it had to be done. She carefully removed the parchment from its frame, then searched through the piles of translations and notes on the kitchen table. Finally she found the Secret Scroll on the chair where Kendra had been sitting the night before. She carried both manuscripts upstairs and set them on her desk.

Next she gathered paints and brushes and sat down. She studied the artwork on the Secret Scroll, then slowly began copying its rich patterns of gold, red, and blue onto Kendra's old manuscript.

It was late afternoon when she finished. She studied her work. She had managed to copy the exotic birds and animals hidden in the foliage on the borders, and even the detailed picture of the goddess locking the jaws of hell. Her work was rough, but at a distance it would fool Toby or any of the Regulators, especially since they were afraid to touch it.

Satisfied, she went to her closet. She searched through her clothes until she found the strapless top with the slit in the front. She slipped it over her head, then grabbed a silky black skirt and stepped into it. She carried her stiletto boots to the bed and tugged them on.

At last she drew black liquid eyeliner over her top lid, added green glitter shadow, rolled thick mascara on her lashes, and brushed her hair. She added gloss to her lips and rubbed sparkle lotion over her arms and chest. Then she remembered the dragon stencils. Soon, she had a sinuous dragon adorning her thigh between the bottom of her skirt and the top of her boots. She liked the look. She turned in front of the full-length mirror behind the bathroom door.

"Dynamite," she whispered. Her reflection thrilled her. She looked vamped-out and mystical. At once, she sensed the fierce power of the dragon rising in her. She felt like an invincible goddess-warrior.

She crept down the hallway and stairs, her heels clicking on the wood floors, then paused over Kendra, who was now curled on the couch, breathing uneasily. She kissed her forehead. The kiss was her seal; tonight she would release Kendra from the curse.

She started to leave when the doorbell rang. She opened the door.

Jimena and Serena stepped inside, their eyes smoky with makeup, star glitter on their arms and cheeks and hair. They were mysterious creatures of the night, now.

"We knew you'd need our help," Jimena said.

"Thanks," Catty answered, smiling.

"She saw you next to a carousel with Toby." Serena seemed unsure. "Does that make sense?"

Catty nodded. "Toby asked me to meet him at the carousel in Griffith Park. He's a Regulator. He's got Vanessa and he won't let her go until I destroy the Secret Scroll." Then Catty told them the details of what had happened.

Neither Jimena nor Serena seemed surprised.

"Do you think all the Regulators will be there?" Serena glanced down at her moon amulet as she opened the door.

"No, just Toby," Catty answered. "I don't think he'll want to share the glory with the others."

Jimena nodded and followed Serena.

Catty stepped outside and saw Jimena's brother's blue-and-white '81 Oldsmobile parked at the curb. That took care of one problem at least. They had transportation.

She glanced up at the Hollywood sign. Smoke billowed into the evening sky, close to the huge white letters. Another fire. It felt like an omen. She suddenly stopped and wondered if they shouldn't turn back.

"*¡Vayamos!*" Jimena squealed and slid behind the steering wheel.

"Come on," Serena called back to Catty. "Let's go."

Catty reluctantly climbed in the backseat. A feeling of foreboding twisted through her as the car shot away from the curb. She hoped she wasn't leading her friends to their deaths.

CHAPTER TWENTY-THREE

HEAT FROM THE DAY intensified the pungent smell of smoke from the fire in the hills near Griffith Park. The acrid fumes stung Catty's eyes and the back of her throat as she stepped away from the car. Overhead, the smoke-clouded sky reflected the setting sun with a golden cast.

"We're early," Jimena announced and jumped on the carousel. She patted the neck of an outside horse and smoothed her hand over the glass jewels set in the bridle, then she threaded her way through the first and second row of ponies. "I used to love riding this carousel," she announced.

"Me, too," Serena agreed. She climbed on and swung her leg over a black steed.

Jimena and Catty laughed as Serena pretended to gallop away, but their laughter suddenly stopped. The silence in the park became over-whelming and the length of Catty's back shivered with anticipation.

Jimena crouched beside a white horse. "What is it?"

The air felt permeated with a negative charge, as it had in the coroner's office when the Regulators had entered the reception area.

"It's Toby," Catty said.

A security light unexpectedly blinked on. In the sudden brightness the wooden horses seemed to come to life. Their glass eyes blazed yellow and their shiny muscles seemed strained, as if the horses were trying to escape from whatever was coming.

"Did he do that?" Serena whispered in awe.

"What?" Catty asked.

"Make the light go on," Jimena spoke in a low voice.

Catty shrugged.

The air became heavier and more electric. The small hairs on her arms rose and her skin prickled.

Then, the carousel creaked and groaned as if struggling against inertia. A cascade of sparks fell from the generator.

Serena let out a soft hiss of air. "Freaky."

"*¿Qué hay que hacer?*" Jimena asked quietly. "Should we be doing anything?"

Catty shook her head. "Wait."

Gears squeaked, and then the horses rose and fell. Serena climbed off hers in quick, jerking motions and stood beside it in awe.

They watched in amazement as the platform circled. Then the band organ pinged. Music sputtered and stopped. A trumpet squawked, then continued to play. Finally, cymbals and drums joined the brass. The horses moved up and down.

Serena and Jimena jumped off the slow-moving carousel and stood with Catty.

After the first rotation the platform circled with ever increasing speed, stirring a breeze that rushed over them. The manuscript flapped back and forth in Catty's hands.

"Stay back," Catty ordered suddenly. "He'll know you're here, but I don't want him to think we came to have a standoff."

Jimena and Serena stepped back until their faces were hidden in darkness.

"Catty," Jimena warned and pointed.

Beneath the bulking trees, purple shadows clustered and grew thicker. Leaves on the bottom branches quivered. Suddenly Catty knew it had been a mistake to come here with the fake manuscript, a foolish, impulsive mistake. How could she fight something whose aura alone was strong enough to give a carousel life? She had put her friends needlessly in danger and there was little chance of success. She turned to tell Jimena and Serena to run; but before she could, the face in the shadows became whole.

Toby emerged in his disguise, holding Vanessa behind him. The whirling lights from the carousel cast a kaleidoscope of everchanging patterns over them. The breeze ruffled Vanessa's hair, but Toby's stayed rigidly in place.

He walked slowly forward. His feet made no sound in the dry grass. He stopped before he reached Catty. His eyes were the same as the wooden horses, lacking warmth and light of their own, but stealing it from the environment and reflecting it back.

"You have it." He glanced at the parchment in her hands but did not come closer to examine it.

Catty held it up. Was it only her imagination or had he glanced away? Could he be that frightened of the manuscript and its curse? But why? He seemed so all-powerful.

"Take off your moon amulet," he ordered.

She hesitated. She never took off her amulet. Was it a trick? She glanced at Vanessa, hoping for some clue. But Vanessa didn't appear to have heard Toby. She didn't seem to even be aware of where she was. She was too deep inside herself. Toby sensed what Catty was thinking and pushed a strand of hair away from Vanessa's face, then bent and kissed her lips.

Vanessa jerked back.

Toby glanced at Catty and smiled. "My beautiful moon goddess doesn't appreciate my kisses now, but she will learn to. Won't you, Vanessa?" He rubbed the back of Vanessa's neck and placed a possessive arm around her.

Vanessa began trembling.

Catty yanked off the moon amulet. "As soon as the manuscript is destroyed, you let Vanessa free."

Toby nudged Vanessa gently. "Go wait under the tree."

She obediently stepped back under the branches.

He turned to Catty, satisfied. "When the moon rises," he commanded, "reflect the light of the moon from your amulet onto the manuscript."

Catty gazed at the night sky. The moon

edged over the jagged tops of the trees. She glanced at Toby to see if the time was right, then lifted the amulet and reflected the milky glow of the moon onto the manuscript. For a moment Catty worried that if Toby looked closely, he would know it wasn't the real Secret Scroll. Then the parchment began to bubble and foam and she relaxed.

At last, a streak of purple light shot from her amulet. The manuscript pulsated, then exploded into a thousand fragments that rained down on the night.

Tiny wisps of white smoke curled in the air where the sparks had been.

Toby smirked.

"Now," Catty shouted.

Serena and Jimena suddenly ran from the shadows. They quickly grabbed Vanessa and pulled her back to Catty.

"Go," Jimena ordered. She and Serena held Vanessa's hands and latched on to Catty's shoulders.

Catty concentrated, trying to use her power

of time travel for them to escape. Instantly, the carousel and trees roared away from them in a blinding shaft of light and they were falling into the tunnel.

Catty whooped as she clasped her moon amulet around her neck. "We did it!"

Jimena yelled, "We fooled him."

"I can't believe it was so easy," Serena added.

Catty looked at Vanessa. Her eyes were blank and she didn't seem to realize where she was. "Do you think Vanessa will be okay?"

"*Claro,*" Jimena reassured her and gave Vanessa's hand to Catty. "We'll take her to Maggie."

Catty clasped Vanessa's hand tightly.

As they drifted deeper into the tunnel, Catty became aware that something was wrong. She glanced down at her watch. The hands had stopped moving. Panic seized her. They were no longer traveling from one time to another but hovering. This had only happened before when she had tried to go too far back into the past.

"What's wrong?" Jimena asked.

"I don't know," Catty answered. And then she felt a presence. She wrenched her head around.

Toby appeared behind her, grinning. "The tunnel is my realm," he said.

Catty struggled to leave the tunnel and fall back into time, but her power wasn't working.

Toby seemed to understand what she was trying to do. "I have even more power here. You can't escape me now."

Catty drew in a huge gulp of air. How was she going to save her friends? She felt as if she had led them into a trap.

Jimena tugged at her. "Drop back into time."

"I can't," Catty answered. "He's not letting me. He has more power than I do."

The tunnel seemed to be heating. Catty could feel beads of perspiration gathering on her forehead.

"Is the tunnel always this hot?" Serena asked.

Catty shook her head. "No. It's Toby. He's building a huge electrical charge."

"Look." Serena pointed.

Blue and orange sparks crackled around the tunnel walls.

"You think he's building a charge so he can zap us with electricity?" Jimena asked.

"Why not?" Catty answered. "We've all gotten electric shocks when he was around."

"But that was static electricity," Serena replied.

"Lightning is the same thing," Catty explained. "Just static electricity suddenly discharging between clouds and the ground."

Jimena turned quickly to Serena. "Maybe you can go into his mind and try to stop him."

"I'll try." Serena concentrated. Her eyes began to dilate and then suddenly her body jerked. "Ouch!" she yelled.

Toby's laughter filled the tunnel.

"What?" Catty and Jimena asked together.

"He shocked me." Serena looked surprised. "It was like hitting an electric fence. He's got some kind of shield."

Catty watched Toby. The smile on his face

told her that he had something horrible planned
for them.

The friends squeezed together and waited
for the end.

CHAPTER TWENTY-FOUR

UNEXPECTEDLY, TOBY grabbed Catty's shoulder. The coldness of his fingers seemed to sink deep inside her, making her body cold in spite of the heat.

"Did you really think you were the only one with the ability to escape into a different dimension?" he sneered.

Catty closed her eyes in concentration and tried one last time to escape the tunnel. This time when she opened her eyes, she was surprised to find herself standing alone in a dreamscape.

Rolling mists circled her feet and the horizon had the same pinkish cast and line of craggy mountains that she remembered from a repeated nightmare. Only now forks of lightning cut across the sky. She knew if she took a step forward she would find herself sucked down into quicksand and suffocated. That was the way it had always happened in her terrifying dream. How many times had she awakened from it, gasping for air? Except now she wasn't dreaming. She was awake.

She cautiously turned. She didn't see her friends.

"Jimena!" she called. "Serena!" Her words echoed peculiarly around her, disturbing the mists as if her voice had become three-dimensional.

When no one answered, she turned back. Were they still in the tunnel? Or without her power, had they been forced back into time? She hoped they were safe.

She stared ahead. Something hidden in the mists was watching her, something malevolent.

The feeling was not new to her. She had felt it in this dream before. Now she wondered if it had always been Toby or one of the other Regulators.

A fine tremor started in her legs and traveled up her spine. She feared what would happen next. She took a deep breath and waited. Was there any way she could exit the nightmare? She had to find some way. If she didn't, Serena and Vanessa and Jimena might be trapped in the tunnel or worse, lost in another time with no way to get back to the present, and it would be her fault.

But she was awake. Maybe that meant she could do something. Perhaps she could turn and run away from the quicksand.

Slowly, she took one step backward. When nothing stopped her, she quickly removed her boots, and then spun around and ran. As she sped across the dreamscape, her steps became lighter, and soon she was sweeping over the dream world like a wind. She felt suddenly optimistic. Maybe because she was awake she would be capable of changing the outcome. If she concentrated hard enough, could she create an opening in the dream?

One that would lead her back to the tunnel?

Without warning, lightning crackled and split the air in front of her. In the jagged light, grotesque faces formed and surged around her. She tried to press through them but she felt herself being turned in the direction of the quicksand. Were these the undisguised faces of the Regulators? She struggled against their roiling faces, but in the end, their strength was too great.

As she was thrust closer and closer to the oozing quicksand, she tried to convince herself that even though she was awake what was happening to her was only an illusion. Nothing here could really hurt her.

She was only inches from the quicksand now. Her heart hammered inside her rib cage. Would she suffocate?

As if to answer her question, Toby abruptly appeared beside her. "I came to watch the end."

His disguise was completely gone now. His face was cruelly distorted, eyes evil and piercing. "This isn't a dream, Catty," he smirked. "If you fall in the quicksand here, you die."

Already she could feel the cold swampy waters lapping at her toes.

She tried to keep her feet from moving but they seemed to have an intent of their own.

"Just one step," his voice urged.

Against her will, her feet inched forward, compelled by Toby's voice. The sucking water and sand swirled around her toes and crept up to her ankles. Immediately, she started to sink as she had done so many times before in the dream.

The slimy waters quickly reached the top of her knees and edged up her thighs.

Her body tensed in an involuntary scream that came painfully and silently from her throat. She pressed her eyes closed against the nightmare and waited for death to take her.

She thought of the manuscript. At least the manuscript hadn't been destroyed. It would be safe until another heir was born. That was the only thing she had managed to do right. She had failed miserably at everything else. If only Serena, Jimena, and Vanessa could be saved.

All at once Toby grabbed her arm. "What

did you say?" His words breathed against her ear and she turned her face away from his fetid smell.

"I said nothing," she answered and watched in horror as the spongy quicksand pulled her deeper and the sandy mire lapped at the top of her thighs.

"About the manuscript," he yelled in frustration. "You said something about the manuscript."

"No." She shook her head.

"In dreams, thoughts are expressed aloud," he warned. "You said *'at least the manuscript hasn't been destroyed.'*"

Toby's monstrous eyes flared and she watched in bewilderment as a jagged hole tore the dreamscape apart.

Suddenly she was back in the tunnel, clasping hands with Jimena and Serena. Jimena was holding Vanessa tightly against her.

"What happened?" Jimena asked.

"He took me into a dream," Catty answered, and before she could say more, they tumbled from the tunnel back into time.

Toby was in a rage. He quickly reworked his

features, changing nose, eyes, and hair until he resembled the schoolboy Toby.

"Where are we?" Jimena stared at the land around them.

"It looks normal enough," Catty examined the nearby eucalyptus trees. "Maybe we're back in Griffith Park." But the feel of the air was too heavy and the silence surrounding them too complete.

"Are we in another dream?" Serena asked and pointed up.

Giant sparks of heat lightning split across the night sky. Terrible thunder followed, shaking the ground beneath them.

Catty shook her head. "I don't know."

Then she saw Vanessa, lying on the ground. She got up and went to her. She knelt beside her, cradled her, and held her tightly. In the flashing glow from the lightning, Vanessa's face looked pallid and sickly. Her eyes no longer focused and her heartbeat felt weak and slow.

Catty stared back at Toby as he paced angrily around them. Nothing was taking Vanessa from her. Not death. Not Toby. But even as she made the promise to herself, she felt Vanessa weaken and slip away. Tenderly she stroked Vanessa's hair and kissed the top of her head.

Toby walked slowly toward her.

CHAPTER TWENTY-FIVE

CATTY STARED AT Toby as he paced silently around her.

"I understand your trickery now," he said.

Catty remained motionless, paralyzed with intense fear, not for herself, but for Vanessa.

His voice was deadly when he spoke again. "You didn't destroy the Secret Scroll."

"I did," Catty lied.

"That was a forgery you destroyed." His hand whipped out and he yanked Vanessa from her arms. Catty threw herself at Toby and tried to pry her from him. Sparks of electricity stung her, but still her fingers worked to free Vanessa.

"Confess," he ordered.

"Let Vanessa go with Jimena and Serena and I'll tell you," she answered.

He smiled mockingly, as if her bravery amused him. He dropped Vanessa, and she crumpled to the ground. Jimena and Serena pulled her away.

"I took another old manuscript and painted it to make it look like the Secret Scroll," Catty admitted. "I didn't think you'd look at it closely."

His eyes narrowed into slits but not before she caught a flicker of uneasiness. "Take me to the real manuscript," he spoke more calmly now.

Catty looked around her. "How? I don't even know where we are."

"Where is the manuscript?" he demanded.

"My house," she said quietly and hoped that Kendra was sleeping. She didn't need to add her into the mix.

He touched her shoulder and her body

began to shiver. "Take the hands of your friends," he ordered.

As soon as she did, lightning flared around them. They were lifted into a vortex of white light and soon they were standing in Catty's backyard.

"Get the manuscript," Toby ordered. "The correct one. No trickery." He pressed one menacing hand around Vanessa's neck in warning.

"I understand." Catty hurried toward her house. But as she walked across the patio and opened the sliding glass door, she remembered what Maggie had told them. Regulators were afraid of the Secret Scroll. There had to be a reason. Something more than the curse. If the Path of the manuscript described the way to vanquish the Atrox, then surely it must also tell how to destroy the Regulators.

She dashed across the kitchen, her heart beating with renewed hope, and climbed the stairs. Maybe the manuscript could protect them!

She walked into her bedroom and started to grab the manuscript from her desk. Her hand stopped in midair.

The manuscript was gone.

She glanced at the hallway. Had Kendra come into her room and taken it? What if she had tried to destroy the manuscript herself? That would be so like Kendra.

Catty rushed down the hallway and paused at the door to Kendra's room. A dim night-light cast an orange glow across the room. Catty entered silently, the thick oriental carpet absorbing her footsteps, and sat on the edge of the bed. Kendra's breathing was thick and heavy. Her eyes opened and she smiled thinly. Catty knew without asking that she was feeling worse.

"I need the manuscript, Kendra," Catty spoke softly. "Where is it?"

"The kitchen." Her breath hitched and broke the words apart. "I was double-checking my translations. I wanted to find some clue."

Catty suddenly remembered the incantation that Kendra had yelled at her the night before. That had to be the answer. She started to ask, but Kendra had fallen back into a deep sleep.

She bolted from the room and ran down the

stairs to the kitchen. She searched quickly through the scribbled pages scattered about the table. Finally she found what she was looking for. The words were underlined in bold red slashes. That was exactly what she needed.

She read it quickly, then grabbed the manuscript and went back outside to face Toby.

CHAPTER TWENTY-SIX

CATTY STEPPED FORWARD, holding the Secret Scroll high in the air as Kendra had done the night before.

Toby glanced at her, a smile of triumph on his face. Then Catty spoke and his smile vanished.

"Demere personam tuam atque ad dominum tuum se referre." Catty recited the incantation clearly. The words empowered her and the Scroll seemed to come to life, its force throbbing through her.

Toby hesitated, then backed up slowly. Blue sparks fluttered around his body.

Catty started to repeat the incantation but before she could, white clouds pushed into her vision. Was he taking her into another dream? She shuddered. He controlled her in the dreamland. Once there, he could force her to destroy the Scroll.

Desperately, she lifted the manuscript and tried to say the words but her voice had become useless. She struggled to speak and now her lips refused to move.

Her vision cleared suddenly and she was back in the same nightmare. The jagged mountains from her dream came into clear focus. Toby stepped through the churning mists.

"You'll never be able to use the incantation in my world," he said with a terrible smile. "Destroy the Secret Scroll."

She forced her lips to move. "I won't destroy it." She was resolute, but already her free hand was reaching for her amulet. As her hand started to yank the amulet from its chain, a searing pain stabbed her back. She looked at Toby to see why he had hurt her, but his eyes looked as confused as she felt.

Another spike of pain dug into her and as it did, the dream broke apart like a thousand birds scattering into flight.

She shook her head. She was standing back in her yard, clutching the manuscript. Jimena and Serena held her arms.

"Sorry." Jimena smiled deviously. "I had to hit you." She rubbed Catty's back.

"We figured pain would jar you out of the dream-trance," Serena explained, massaging Catty's shoulder.

Toby glared at them and took a step forward.

"Thanks, I guess." Catty grinned in spite of the pain twisting through her.

Toby took another trudging step toward them.

"Here," Catty whispered and pointed to the lines in the manuscript. "Maybe we'll have more power if we say the incantation together."

They grasped the manuscript and repeated the incantation after Catty. *"Demere personam tuam atque ad dominum tuum se referre."*

A brilliant white flash stung their eyes and

filled the yard with a strange light. Then another flare as bright as lightning roared around Toby.

"We did it!" Serena squealed and let go of the manuscript.

"Wait," Catty cautioned. "Something feels wrong." And then she knew. They hadn't destroyed Toby. He was escaping into the tunnel.

Before they could react, Toby grabbed Vanessa and took her with him.

"No!" Catty screamed.

"Follow him," Jimena yelled.

"Hold on to me," Catty ordered.

Jimena and Serena grabbed onto Catty's arms, then she opened the tunnel and they fell in after Toby and Vanessa. Catty was going dangerously fast but she needed to catch up to them. She wouldn't be able to go as far back in time as Toby could go, so her only chance to save Vanessa was now.

"Say the words together," Catty urged and held up the manuscript.

Jimena and Serena each put one hand on the manuscript while their other hand clasped Catty tightly. Then they repeated the incantation.

Finally, Jimena stopped. *"Mira."* She pointed.

Toby's appearance began to change. His features twisted and melted. His mouth stretched into a brutal slash of scar tissue. Cartilage curled irregularly around two holes where his nose had been. He crouched over, his breathing labored. Air rattled from his throat. What remained of him seemed to fall into a deep sleep. Toby began to tumble away from them, carrying Vanessa with him.

"We have to save Vanessa!" Jimena shouted. "Catch up to him."

"I don't know if I can," Catty answered, straining her power.

"Try," Serena yelled.

Vanessa stirred.

"Vanessa!" Catty yelled.

Vanessa glanced at her weakly, then a baffled look crossed her face. She seemed to become aware of her surroundings again. She gasped when she saw the monstrous creature who was holding her. She struggled to free herself from the clawlike hands but they held her tightly. She reached toward Catty.

Catty grabbed Vanessa and wrenched her free. As she did, the manuscript fell from her hands.

Jimena started to go after it.

"Don't," Catty warned. "If you let go of me, you'll fall back into time, and who knows where you'll land."

"I wish you'd mentioned that earlier." Serena held more tightly to Catty's arm.

They watched the Secret Scroll fall into the void and disappear. Then they landed back in time.

"Where are we?" Serena asked and looked around. "I hope this is real life and not someone's dream."

CHAPTER TWENTY-SEVEN

Catty looked up at the hills and saw the Hollywood sign. "We're in L.A.," she answered with a surge of happiness.

"When?" Jimena asked urgently and looked around her.

"Yeah," Serena wondered. "What day is it?"

Catty glanced down at her watch and looked at the date display. "It's the same night we left."

"Great, let's go get the car," Serena suggested.

"Yeah," Jimena said. "Then let's get something to eat. *Tengo hambre.*"

"Isn't anyone going to tell me what's going on?" Vanessa asked. "What was that monster?"

"You tell her," Serena told Catty.

"It's a long story," Catty began as they started walking toward a bus stop.

An hour later, they were in Jimena's car, driving through the park. Cool air smelling of pine and eucalyptus rushed through the windows. The fires had been put out and the winds from the ocean had driven the smoke away.

Catty rested her head on the backseat and looked out at the night.

"I almost got us all destroyed," Vanessa remarked. "None of this would have happened if I hadn't been trying to make Michael jealous." She shook her body. "Yuck. Did you see what Toby really looked like?"

Catty nodded. "A putrid monster. I tried to tell you."

"We all did," Jimena put in.

Vanessa sighed and looked out the window. "Tell me I didn't kiss him when he looked like that."

"You kissed him," Catty teased.

"No way." Vanessa covered her face.

"Yes way," Serena laughed.

"With tongue," Jimena added with glee.

"I wonder what Michael is doing tonight?" Vanessa leaned back against the seat and laughed. "I hope I didn't make him too jealous."

They all laughed.

"I got my one and only," Jimena remarked. "Collin *es mi todo*. Only two more days and he'll be back from Hawaii."

"I had my guy," Catty sighed. "Too bad."

Serena turned and looked at her. "You're not going to break up with Chris, are you?"

"He's so cool," Jimena added. "You'll be sorry."

Vanessa smiled slyly. "Wait until you hear about Chris."

"What's with Chris now?" Serena asked.

"Well, he's a few hundred years old for one thing," Vanessa began.

Then Catty explained.

By the time Catty arrived home, Kendra was up, sitting at the kitchen table in her robe and big furry slippers.

"I must have been delirious," she said. "I hope I didn't frighten you."

Catty shook her head.

Kendra's hand sifted through the piles of papers on the table. "You'll never believe the things I thought I read in that manuscript." She paused, her eyes fearful, and looked at Catty. "It was all true, wasn't it?"

Catty hesitated, wondering if she should tell Kendra the truth.

Then Kendra took her hand and Catty began to speak. There was a lot she still didn't understand, but what she knew, she told her.

CHAPTER TWENTY-EIGHT

AFTER SCHOOL ON Monday, Catty sat alone in the kitchen. Memories from the days before weighed down on her. There was no awakening from what had happened but it felt more like a nightmare now than real. It had been difficult to sleep and she felt tired. She wondered how long the fear of dreaming would stay with her.

Shadows stretched and seemed to move and shift as if the setting sun were giving them life. Catty looked behind her, trying to reassure herself that there was nothing in the dark but her own imagination. Toby and the manuscript were gone. She was safe.

For a moment she imagined she heard someone walking slowly in the living room. She tensed and listened intently. Then she caught movement in the corner of her eye. She gasped.

When she turned, Chris stepped out of the doorway and into the fading light. His smile delighted her. He was beautiful, and yet there was a difference in his appearance, a confidence and strength that he no longer had to hide.

She felt surprised and happy to see him.

"I can't stay long." He sat beside her. "I have to find the manuscript."

"Sorry. It's all my fault."

"Sorry?" He shook his head. "You protected the manuscript and saved Vanessa. You did the right thing."

He stared at her, a look of longing in his eyes, and she knew intuitively that he liked her as much as she liked him. It was more than like, it was a deep friendship with mutual respect, but sadly she knew that they could never have a relationship.

But she did know she wanted one last kiss. She leaned forward, wondering if she dared kiss him.

He stood suddenly and she pulled back abruptly. "Sorry," she whispered as a blush spread across her face.

"About what now?" he asked softly and then he took her hand and pulled her up against him. He looked down at her and smiled. It was a warm smile, but with an air of sadness.

She sighed. She would never meet anyone so perfect for her again. His hand brushed through her hair.

"We'll be together again someday," he assured her, and she knew it wasn't a wish but a promise.

Then his lips were on hers and he held her tightly.

"Someday," she whispered.

SISTERS
of
ISIS

The Summoning

Sudi had spent the afternoon ripping up all of her pictures of Brian. She wanted zero reminders of him. But now she wondered if maybe the break-up with Brian was affecting her more than she wanted to admit. Brian had scared her. Did he still? Could anxiety have caused her sleepwalking?

She grabbed the masking tape from her desk drawer and tore off several pieces, then stuck them over the doorjamb and across the door. The tape wouldn't stop her from leaving her room, but she hoped that untangling it would be enough to awaken her if she did start sleepwalking again. She crawled into bed, wanting nothing more than to huddle under her covers and lose herself in dreams. Pie jumped on the quilt, curled up beside her, and began purring noisily.

As Sudi drifted off, she thought of Brian again. They had broken up on Saturday, but the real break had come the day Dominique Dupont had transferred into Lincoln High School. Her father was the cultural attaché at the French embassy. Usually the diplomats' kids attended Entre Nous Academy, but Dominique had wanted to experience the "real" American teen life, so she had enrolled in public school.

Sudi shuddered, trying to push memories of Brian away. She should have felt grateful that they were through, so why did she keep on crying? It wasn't as if she had really been crazy about Brian, anyway. She had liked Scott, but Brian had asked her out first, and by her third date with Brian, everyone was calling them a couple.

Then Brian had revealed a darker side, and

everything about their relationship had changed. What had made her go back for more?

She drifted off, her mind replaying the memory of the night she wanted to forget.

* * *

LYNNE EWING Lynne Ewing is a screenwriter who also counsels troubled teens. In addition to writing all of the Daughters of the Moon books, she is also the author of the popular companion series Sons of the Dark, as well as the new series Sisters of Isis. Ms. Ewing lives in Washington, DC.